Curvy in College
The Jock and the Genius

BY

Annabelle Winters

Copyright Notice

Cover Design by S. Lee

ISBN: 9798670085717

0 1 2 3 4 5 6 7 8 9

Books by Annabelle Winters

The CURVES FOR SHEIKHS Series
Curves for the Sheikh
Flames for the Sheikh
Hostage for the Sheikh
Single for the Sheikh
Stockings for the Sheikh
Untouched for the Sheikh
Surrogate for the Sheikh
Stars for the Sheikh
Shelter for the Sheikh
Shared for the Sheikh
Assassin for the Sheikh
Privilege for the Sheikh
Ransomed for the Sheikh
Uncorked for the Sheikh
Haunted for the Sheikh
Grateful for the Sheikh
Mistletoe for the Sheikh
Fake for the Sheikh

The CURVES FOR SHIFTERS Series
Curves for the Dragon
Born for the Bear
Witch for the Wolf
Tamed for the Lion
Taken for the Tiger

The CURVY FOR HIM Series
The Teacher and the Trainer
The Librarian and the Cop
The Lawyer and the Cowboy
The Princess and the Pirate

The CEO and the Soldier
The Astronaut and the Alien
The Botanist and the Biker
The Psychic and the Senator

THE CURVY FOR THE HOLIDAYS SERIES
Taken on Thanksgiving
Captive for Christmas
Night Before New Year's
Vampire's Curvy Valentine
Flagged on the Fourth
Home for Halloween

THE CURVY FOR KEEPS SERIES
Summoned by the CEO
Given to the Groom

THE DRAGON'S CURVY MATE SERIES
Dragon's Curvy Assistant
Dragon's Curvy Banker
Dragon's Curvy Counselor
Dragon's Curvy Doctor
Dragon's Curvy Engineer
Dragon's Curvy Firefighter
Dragon's Curvy Gambler

WWW.ANNABELLEWINTERS.COM

Curvy in College
The Jock and the Genius

BY

Annabelle Winters

1
<u>LOGAN</u>

It's called *Rocks for Jocks*," whispers some freckle-faced freshman passing by the Geology 101 classroom. "All the dumb-ass meatheads major in Geology coz it's easy."

I glance over at Freckle-face, my left eyebrow raised, right fist clenched. He's got a highly punchable face, it occurs to me as I break him down to a nervous puddle with one look. I'm at least a foot taller than him, and although I'm not above breaking someone's nose just for the hell of it, this kid looks like he's still a few years away from puberty. I might kill him without even meaning to, and manslaughter charges won't help me get my grades back to where I can keep my athletic scholarships.

So I let the little worm wriggle away and turn my attention back to my first class of Fall Semester. It's my Junior Year—though just barely. I shoulda failed three classes last year, but instead I pulled the old trick of withdrawing before the profs could fail my ass. Shoulda known better than to buck the trend among athletes—which is why I'm becoming a*Rocks-for-Jocks* major.

"Don't overthink it, Logan. Just fucking major in Geology like the rest of you athletes," my suitemate Mason had told me after Freshman Year, when it became clear that I wasn't the sharpest tool in the shed, no matter how tight I ran my wide-receiver routes on the football field, no matter how true I could aim that fastball over the plate, no matter how fast I could blaze around the corner on my way to breaking the Weston University record in the 400 meters (for the second time, btw . . . half the track records are now owned by yours truly, so I'm really just competing against myself these days).

If I'd listened to Mason two years ago I'd be taking the advanced Geology classes by now, breezing through the system with the guys from the football and baseball teams. But I'm a late-bloomer, and now I'm starting a new major the beginning of my Junior Year—which means I'm surrounded by freshmen in this intro class.

I nod at a couple of new ballers I met during practice earlier, but I make no effort to go sit by them. I get along just fine with the guys on the teams, but I don't typically hang out with them outside of practice. Maybe it's because I'm not a one-sport athlete. I can kill it on the football field, the baseball diamond, and my favorite: The open track in the stadium. There's nothing like the rush you get when you're running with everything you've got, experiencing the purest form of human physicality.

Though maybe there's another form of human physicality as pure and magnificent, I think as I slide into a seat by the door and stretch my long arms over both the adjoining chairs, manspreading like my balls have the right of way in here. I shamelessly check out a group of first-year women, reveling in how they get all self-conscious as they walk past me. A couple of them are cute, but overall this year's class doesn't seem to have much to offer. Yeah, there's always the groupie-chicks who hang out at football and baseball practice, but that doesn't interest me these days. Couple years ago I was like a stallion out of control, but lately I've been on this kick of saving up my sexual energy.

I read something about how professional boxers would go months without sex when they were training for a big fight. Some of the champions wouldn't even jerk off. It was monk-like shit, but I thought I'd try it anyway. I'm always looking to get an edge. Find a new way to dominate everyone around me.

So I took the summer off from sex, and I sure as

hell noticed a big difference in my performance on the field. I was always the fastest guy on the football field, but now my route-running is tighter, my footwork is better, my vision is clearer. In baseball I'm putting the ball exactly where I want it, and my arm doesn't get tired as easily. As for track . . . well, I broke my own 200m record yesterday just running at 80% effort in practice!

Yeah, so the no-sex shit really does work. But it has some side-effects, I think as I pan the classroom and pick up nothing but tits and thighs, smell nothing but pussy. I'm at peak fitness right now, and my body is yearning to spread its seed, just like evolution wants. Maybe those monks found a way to peacefully suppress their needs, but I'm so fucking horny I'm having wet dreams like I'm twelve years old again!

"Watch yourself, Logan," I growl under my breath when I realize I'm getting hard even though there's no one particularly interesting in the classroom. "Walking around with a loaded gun is dangerous. Take one wrong step and—"

"That's *so* wrong. You're taking up *three* chairs. Is there a reason you're taking up three chairs?"

I whip my head around at the sharp tone of a young woman's voice, and when I look up I do a double take.

"Who the hell are you?" I say, my gaze immediately taking in every curvy inch of the girl's strong hourglass shape. She's got big brown eyes, big round boobs, and nice wide hips that I want to hold down firmly in my bed as I take her deep and hard. She's dressed in a frilly white blouse and baggy blue jeans like her grandmother, though, and I wonder if she's wearing old-fashioned panties pulled up past her belly-button.

"That's not a relevant question," she says firmly, touching the bridge of her nose like she normally wears glasses. "You can't be taking up three chairs in a classroom. It's disrespectful."

I lazily glance around the classroom, taking my time just to see if I can make this firecracker of a first-year even more pissed off. I gesture with my head towards a couple of seats in the far corner.

"There's a couple chairs over there," I drawl, spreading my arms out wider, parting my legs even more, making no attempt to hide my bulge that's bordering on obscene. "These are all taken, kid."

"Kid?" she says, frowning and placing a hand on her hip as I try not to imagine my own hand sliding down her mom-jeans that I really think might be hand-me-downs from like three generations of her family. "I'm an adult woman, and you'll treat me with respect."

I grin and look up at her, locking in on her eyes until she blinks and looks away. "You gotta earn my respect, kiddo," I say, narrowing my green eyes at her when she dares to attempt to re-engage. "And all you've done so far is yell at me for being disrespectful when

I'm sitting here minding my own damned business."

"You can mind your own business on one chair instead of three," she says. "Now please move or I'll tell the professor."

I laugh so hard I almost fall off my chair. "Since when do adult women complain to teacher?" I say through a taunting grin.

The girl turns bright red, and I see that's she's mortified for setting me up for a perfect comeback. She touches her dark hair and looks past me towards those seats way in the back. I can tell she doesn't want to sit in the back. She's a front-row kinda gal. I'm surprised she didn't bring a fucking apple for the professor.

"Meathead," she mutters under her breath as she jostles her way towards those seats all the way in the back. "Don't wanna sit next to you anyway. I might catch whatever disease you have that makes you dumber than the rocks we're going to study in this class."

My neck hairs bristle and my body tightens as I fight to keep from leaping up and saying something that'll really sting. Somehow I contain myself, bottling up the anger so I can use it on the playing field later. I do turn in her direction, though, and when I see her ass move from behind, I'm struck by how attracted I am to this big-hipped bombshell in mom-jeans.

"That smart ass needs a good spanking," I mutter as

I watch her navigate those hips between the narrow aisles until she gets to the last row. She sighs and tosses her books onto the desk before sliding her beautiful body into the chair, and I grunt and look away.

It's almost nine, and Professor Johnson walks in with a stack of handouts. He's a big, burly guy. Used to play left tackle here at Weston back in the day. He was pretty good, I hear. Not good enough for the NFL, but then again, Weston University doesn't send a lot of players to the pros. Or any, for that matter.

Professor Johnson grunts out a welcome and starts to lecture, and I glance back over at that wise-ass girl, a weird restlessness rising up in me as I focus on the empty chair next to her. That girl really got my blood boiling, and the mixture of anger and arousal is a powerful draw.

Professor Johnson's just getting warmed up with stories of tectonic plates and continental drift, and suddenly I spring up from my seat, grab my stuff, and stride to the back of the classroom. Every head in the room turns to me, and even the professor hesitates as my tall, powerful frame dominates everyone's attention.

The girl stares at me as I approach, glancing frantically towards the professor and then looking back at me like she's in mortal fear for her life. I let her squirm as I drop my books on the empty desk right next to hers, and then I break into my killer smile.

"That was a pretty classy insult you hurled at me a

minute ago," I whisper as murmurs rise in the classroom. Everyone knows who I am, of course. And no
doubt they're wondering what the hell I'm doing chat-
ting up an obnoxious know-it-all who's dressed like
it's 1986.

"I'm surprised you're smart enough to figure out it
was an insult," she whispers back, keeping her eyes
focused on the whiteboard.

"You don't know when to stop, do you?" I growl.
"Do you even know who I am?"

"An escaped lab animal from the Science Depart-
ment?" she quips, the corners of her pretty mouth
quivering as she holds back a smile.

I pretend to cough so I can stifle my laugh. Shit,
this girl is sharp like a tack. She's also got this mix of
self-consciousness and self-confidence that's intrigu-
ing, intoxicating, maybe even irresistible. Oh yeah,
and that ass fits the description too.

"That's a pretty good one-liner . . . for third grade,"
I shoot back.

"Yeah, when I saw you I assumed this *was* third
grade," she says without missing a beat.

I'm cracking up, but I can't back down from this
little duel. So I pull out the big guns to see how she
handles herself.

"Your mom called," I whisper. "She wants her jeans
back."

The girl's mouth hangs open and she swallows a
shot of air that makes her burp. I generally don't make

fun of a woman's appearance—though this was technically her clothes, not her looks. Still, I know how to get under a woman's skin, and this is most definitely one way to do it. What'cha gonna do, little girl? Fight back or run away?

"A mosquito called," she says after catching her breath. "It wants its brain back."

I can tell she's still annoyed at that insult about her jeans, but I'm impressed that she hung in there and delivered a solid comeback. My competitiveness and dominance plays out in every aspect of my life, and even most guys end up backing down to me in an argument. As for the girls . . . most are so kicked that I'm even talking to them that they turn into giggly schoolgirls who barely pose any challenge to my relentless teasing.

This girl, though . . . she's *all* challenge.

And man do I relish a challenge.

2
<u>LARA</u>

It's a challenge to stay focused on the lecture when this excruciatingly annoying guy is whispering all kinds of nonsense. I should ignore him, but for some reason I can't help but engage. It doesn't help that he's a towering wall of lean muscle with green eyes that make me feel funny between my legs.

I shift on the cool wooden chair, pulling at the high neckline of my white blouse. The asshole made me all self-conscious about my clothes, and I glance down at my jeans that are pulled up all the way to my boobs. They also flare out at the hips, making me look even wider than I already am. I've always been more comfortable wearing loose clothing, but now I'm wondering if maybe I should use some of that scholarship money to upgrade my wardrobe.

But then I realize that I'm totally reacting to that comment. Why should I suffocate my body in tight clothing just because some rude-ass boy passed a rude-ass remark?! I'm not here to look good. I'm not here to meet boys or to get high or to do stupid shit like you're supposed to in college. I'm here to graduate in two years so I can move on to a PhD program and change the world. Boyfriends, husbands, and family can all wait their turn. I *can't* get distracted this early in my journey. Certainly can't get distracted by a jock with more intelligence in his balls than his head.

Imagine the kids we'd have, I think as I steal a sideways glance at him and shift in my seat again as that tingle between my legs gets harder to ignore. Still, I know enough about biochemistry to know that I'm entering the most fertile period of my life, and this is just my body acting out its dumb destiny. The human body doesn't care about long-term goals and visions to change the world. It only cares about three things. The three F's, I call them.

Feed when you're hungry.

Flee when you're scared.

And fu—

"Fuck me," groans the guy, slamming his phone down on the table and groaning again. He looks over at me and shakes his head. "You're bad luck, you know that?"

I try to ignore him, but it actually looks like something is up. The professor turns his back to the class just then, and I sigh and meet his gaze.

"Bad luck? I've heard that before," I say with an eye-roll. Then I frown at his phone. "We're supposed to turn our phones off during class."

"How do I turn *you* off?" he mutters, flashing a half-smile as he rubs his brutally masculine jaw and blinks like whatever message he got is fighting me for his attention. "Anyway, I forgot there's a football meeting right now. That happens when you're on three teams. So I gotta roll. Nice playing with you, little girl. But recess is over."

I watch as he gathers his stuff and makes like he's about to simply walk out of the room. "You call me little girl again and I swear I'll—"

He stops me with a wickedly triumphant look that makes me squirm. "Actually this is the first time I've called you that. You must be thinking of someone else."

"Must be," is all I manage to say as he straightens up his long, lean body and looks down at me. "Good luck with your meeting," I say awkwardly.

He raises an eyebrow. "Why do I need luck for a meeting?"

I shrug like I don't care. "OK. So you don't need luck. Good luck anyway."

"Girl who brings me bad luck wishing me good luck," he says with a head-shake. "What's your name?"

I blink up at him, touching my hair and blinking again. "Lara," I whisper.

"I'm Logan," he says with a wink. "See you around, yeah?"

"Well, this class meets again on Wednesday," I say. "So I guess I'll see you then."

"Save me a seat, little Lara," he whispers before turning and strolling confidently past the rows of desks, knocking a couple of empty chairs out of the way. He nods at the taken-aback professor, and then he's gone like a mirage over the hot sands of Arabia.

Little Lara, I think as I settle back down and try to pick up on what the professor's saying. Nobody's ever called me little. And although it should be insulting, I *am* kind of little compared to that wall of muscle called Logan.

I smile and sigh as I focus on the professor, who himself is a large man though his mass is mostly flab. He was once muscular, though, I think when the professor turns to the whiteboard and I see his broad back. Maybe he played football during his own college days. Makes sense that he's teaching Geology. After all, my roommate Milly did say that Geology is called *Rocks for Jocks*.

"Aren't you a Biophysics and Genetics major?" Milly had asked. "Why are you taking Geology?"

"I am a Genetics major. But I still need enough credits if I want to graduate in two years, so I'm taking a double courseload every semester," I'd replied. "Geo 101 fits my schedule and seems easy enough that I can get an A without putting in much effort."

Milly had rolled her eyes. "That applies to any class with you," she'd said. "You aced your SATs, didn't you?"

I was surprised she knew, but I'm used to people talking about my achievements. I just shrugged and took the compliment. "Yes," I'd said. "Though that was four years ago. I heard the SATs are tougher now."

"Wait, you took the SATs when you were *fourteen*?" Milly had asked, eyebrows raised, mouth open.

I'd shrugged again. "I was taking college-level AP classes when I was thirteen," I'd said matter-of-factly. "At fifteen I'd already been accepted to Weston U with a full ride."

"So why did it take you three years to get here?" Milly'd asked.

And I'd shaken my head and walked out of the dorm room. I didn't want to go down that road just then. Memory lane is closed. The past is dead. Only the future counts now.

"In the future please keep the chatter to a minimum, Lara," the Professor says as I walk past him on my way to the door after the class wraps up. "I know you're smarter than everyone else in the room put together, but this is my classroom and I expect every student—no matter how gifted—to be respectful when I'm conducting a lecture."

I look at him, surprised that he knows my name. I smile politely and nod, but I don't apologize. This isn't grade school, I want to say. We're all adults here.

"Though I have to say, I'd have thought you'd be smarter than to get involved with someone like Logan," the Prof says from behind me, stopping me cold in my tracks.

I turn slowly, hugging my books against my boobs. "Um, what?"

"I know how cliché this sounds, but he's bad news, Lara," Professor Johnson says, glancing around the now-empty classroom and taking a step towards me. "You have a bright future ahead of you, and you don't need a distraction like Logan screwing things up for you. And believe me, he *will* screw things up for you. Consider yourself warned."

I frown and take a step back. Did I just get transported back to middle school or something? I don't like the vibe I'm getting from the professor, and all this sounds way too personal to be appropriate. Why would he think I'm *involved* with Logan? And what gives him the right to even care, let alone say anything?!

I'm more than capable of challenging him and putting him in his damned place. And I'm certainly capable of going above his head and complaining to one of the Deans. I don't take kindly to being pushed around, and I can push back with the best of them. But this is my first week in college, and if I have a fault, it's that I can sometimes be extremely condescending to teachers. It was a real problem back in middle school, when I was smarter than most of my teachers. I had to tone it down and learn what I could from each teacher before leaving them in my intellectual dust as I moved on to bigger and brighter things.

Anyway, I guess I *was* whispering to Logan, and I suppose that *was* a bit disrespectful. Maybe I cut Professor Johnson some slack and assume the best of intentions.

"Or maybe I just cut this class," I mutter as I step out into the hallway and check my schedule. "I don't actually need to take Geology. I just need any old credit to balance out my science and math classes. It's the first week, and we're allowed two weeks to finalize which classes to take. Yup. That's what I'll do. It's probably more trouble than it's worth, anyway."

But what about Logan, I wonder as I blend in with the clusters of students streaming in and out of classrooms. Is he really more trouble than he's worth?

That tingle teases its way through me again, and I glance at a group of super-stylish sophomores in designer skinny jeans and expensive tights and makeup that makes my eyes hurt. I wouldn't know how to make myself up like that if my life depended on it. Thank goodness it doesn't.

But I can't help but feel a sense of regret that I missed out on those years in high school when girls were learning about make-up and hair and which jeans made their butts look cute. I was always too busy for that, always taking extra classes, always in a hurry to move on, to move up . . .

To grow up.

3
<u>TWO DAYS LATER</u>
<u>LOGAN</u>

"**O**h, grow up," I snarl at a petrified freshman as I push his books off the desk in front of me and use his chair as a foot-rest. I watch as he turns red from suppressing his anger, and I get a dark satisfaction when he skulks away to an open seat on the far side of the classroom.

The rest of the class shoot furtive glances at me and then pretend to talk amongst themselves. I know they think I'm a bully, but I don't give a fuck. I'm in a foul mood, and God help anyone who pushes my buttons today.

Funny thing is, I was in a *great* mood just a few minutes ago—just before I walked into the Geo 101 classroom and didn't see Lara. I'd been thinking about that girl for two days straight, and I've never looked forward to going to class as much as I did this morning. I don't know what it is about her, but everything about her is getting to me.

The way she dresses like she doesn't care what people think. The way she talks like a crazy-smart comedian. Those big brown eyes that blaze with intelligence. That angelic round face that's smooth like a girl's but somehow still projects a maturity that's beyond her years. Fuck, she makes every other girl I've been with feel like a cardboard cutout, a soulless mannequin, just a placeholder until the real thing came along.

"So where the hell is she?" I growl, snapping a pencil with one hand and then tossing the splinters onto the floor like a sulky kid. I glance at my watch. I glance at my phone. I'm wired and restless, and no way I can sit through Professor Johnson explaining how gravel forms or whatever the hell today's lecture is about.

The clock strikes nine, and just as Professor Johnson walks in, I walk out. I came here to see Lara, and I'm pissed she skipped class. Hell, maybe she even dropped it! Why? Did I read her wrong? Does she think I'm a dick? Yeah, she was a little annoyed to begin with, but I can turn on the charm when I want. I could swear we had a great vibe going on Monday. That back and forth was so exciting. I've never felt that kind of electric energy just trading wisecracks with a girl. She's gotten into my head, and I can't get her out.

"You outta here, Logan?" comes Professor Johnson's loud voice from behind me. "I suppose you're ahead of the class anyway, seeing that you're the only Junior in an Introductory course. Wait, are you even a junior this year?"

I whip around to face Johnson, and my body tightens as I rise up to full height. Johnson's a big mother, but I'm an inch taller and packed with hard muscle compared to his soft bulk. The crushing disappointment of not seeing Lara after building it up in my head for two days has got me on edge, and I have to count to ten just to stand down from saying something incredibly stupid. I'm on thin ice with my scholarships as it is, and getting into it with a Professor in my new major probably isn't helpful.

"I don't feel so good, Professor," I mutter, diverting my gaze so he doesn't see that I'm focused like an arrow but not on this bullshit class.

"What is it with you, Logan?" Johnson says, crossing his thick arms over his big belly and sighing. "You think you're gonna make it to the pros or something? Weston is Division III, big shot. You have a better chance of winning the Nobel Prize in Math than catching a pass in the NFL. Your athletic skills got you a free shot at a college education, but you have no appreciation for the chance you've been given. You need to grow up, Logan. Stop acting like a boy and at least *try* to be a man."

"A man like you?" I snap, my anger taking over even though I know it's a bad idea. "Twenty years removed from your glory days? Which weren't even that glorious, from what I hear."

I wince when I feel the insult cut Johnson like a knife. If we were alone, this would have turned into a brawl. I must be insane for getting into it with a Professor in front of an entire class of freshmen who are probably already spreading the word on Social Media. Yup. I can see that kid I bullied excitedly typing away on his phone. I hope he got a good picture of me.

"You done?" says Johnson quietly. His voice is calm, but his eyes are like glowing coals as he fixes his gaze on me until I decide it's time for me to go.

I nod, doing my best to mumble an apology. I manage to get the words out, but I know the damage is done. After this public argument, every Professor at Weston is gonna be on my ass in every class I take with them. I won't be able to skip classes, get extensions on my term papers, get cut some slack for my contributions to the athletic scene on campus. That's gonna make my last two years very hard—if I can still graduate in two years!

"Maybe she is bad luck," I growl to myself as I storm down the hall and push open the side door to one of the stairwells.

And as if the universe agrees with me, my ears almost explode from the shrill sound of an alarm. I turn and stare, almost smacking myself in the head when I realize I just walked out through an emergency exit.

4
LARA

"Now what emergency?" I mutter, checking my phone between classes and seeing the message from my roommate Milly. We get along great, but I've noticed a couple of strange things about her. For one, she's been skipping a lot of classes. Also, she doesn't leave the room much. Like*never* leaves the room.

Milly wants me to pick up the class handouts for the morning classes she skipped. I sigh and shake my head, but I dutifully head for the third floor where the faculty keep their offices. I glance at my phone again to see which classes Milly missed, and I stop just past an open door as I scroll to find her message.

"Yeah, I'm all for having a casual, friendly rapport with students," comes a man's voice from inside the office. "But there needs to be some kind of recognition and respect for authority. Back in the day you called a professor Sir or Ma'am. Now they just use first names like we're their fucking friends! The video's spread all over campus, and I look like a damned fool. It's humiliating as hell. I want action to be taken. You need to make an example out of Logan. I don't care what. Expel his ass, is what I say! Well, yes. I understand that he's the reason we're a Division III school that sells out every football and baseball game all season. Right. The tracks meets too. I understand, but—"

I peek into the office, and realize it's Professor Johnson talking on the phone. He's got his back to the open door, and I can see him clenching and releasing his right fist as he nods and listens. I don't know who's on the other end of the line, but it sounds like someone higher up the ladder.

"What about academic probation?" Johnson says, lowering his voice. "I know he pulled that old trick of withdrawing from three classes last year so he wouldn't have to take the failing grades. But you're only allowed to do that three times, so he's used up his chances. He fails one class this semester and you have to put him on probation, by rule. The moment he goes on probation, all his athletic scholarships get revoked. He isn't a silver-spoon kid. His dad's a garbageman, for heaven's sake! Yeah, Logan fails one class, he'll lose his scholarships, won't be able to afford tuition, and will have to drop out of Weston. What's that? No. Of course not. Wouldn't *dream* of failing him in my class. No siree!"

Johnson chuckles like whoever's on the other line is in tacit agreement, and I'm frozen in place as I listen. I feel like a spy who just overheard a villain planning world domination, and I try to shake the twisty feeling in my gut as I creep back from the open door and hurry away down the hall, doing my best not to run for my life. It was wrong to eavesdrop, but I didn't really mean to do it. That makes it OK, right?

Breathlessly I grab Milly's handouts from the basket outside her professor's office, and I scurry back to the elevators like a thief in the night. It takes forever for the elevator to arrive, and when the door opens and I step in, I'm startled by a lumbering presence behind me.

"Hi, Lara," says Professor Johnson, holding the doors open with his big hands as I stare up at him petrified that he saw me listening. A wave of panic goes through me, and I imagine some horrible scenario where Professor Johnson needs to silence the witness or something creepy like that. "You here to see me?"

"No," I say, smiling awkwardly as I wave Milly's handouts in his face. "My roommate doesn't leave our room much, so I just stopped by to grab these for her."

Johnson grunts and nods, looking me over and then releasing the elevator doors. They close slowly and ominously, and when I'm finally alone I almost burst into tears even though there's no logical reason for it. I'm an expert at handling anxiety, and I only get stronger under pressure, but my heart's beating like a group of bucket-drummers going nuts on the street.

I burst out of the building and take gulping breaths of the fresh fall air. I'm almost knocked over by three big guys rushing into the building, and I quickly step to the side so I don't get crushed by the next wave.

"Hey," comes a voice from my left, and I squint into the bushes and see a long-haired guy smoking something. "You want some?"

I frown and then gasp when I smell the telltale pungency of marijuana. I've never tried it, of course—and I sure as hell have no interest in trying it in the middle of the day out in the open!

"No, thanks," I say, smiling politely and turning away from the guy. "I have to go to class."

"This'll make class more fun," he drawls through a lopsided grin. "Go on. Take a puff."

He holds out the joint but I shake my head and turn away from him again, this time more pointedly. I've been in college for less than a week, and already I'm feeling overwhelmed and totally out of my comfort zone. I'm still processing what I overhead outside Professor Johnson's office, and I'm debating whether I should say something to Logan.

I think about what I just learned about Logan: That he doesn't come from money, that his dad's a garbage-man, that he's dangerously close to losing his scholarships. Oh, and he's got a target on his back thanks to his big ego and even bigger mouth.

"We all have to learn hard lessons," I mutter to myself. "Maybe Logan needs to learn his lesson. Or maybe he just needs to not fail his darned classes! Isn't that what college is about? Not failing your classes?!"

"If you're already talking to yourself, it's probably best you don't get high," comes that long-haired dude's voice through my private rant. He takes the last drag and tosses the joint away just as I turn back to him. "Just messin' with ya. Anyway, I gotta run to class. But if you aren't doing anything later, my band's playing in the Student Union, down in the basement. Swing by with your friends. Free beer for the first set. You got a fake ID?"

I shake my head dumbly. Is he hitting on me? If so, why would he tell me to bring my friends? I look into his eyes, but he's too stoned to focus, and although my knowledge of dating and romance is pretty much zero, I definitely don't get the hitting-on-you vibe. He just wants to fill up the room for his band, I guess.

"My name's Mason," he says just as his phone beeps. "Just a sec," he mutters, checking his phone and cursing out loud. "Goddamn it, Logan. I love you like a brother, but you can be such an obnoxious prick." He glances up at me and shakes his head.

"Sorry. My roommate's in the news again for picking a fight with a Professor."

"You're Logan's roommate?" I blurt out, blinking as my heart pounds from the weird coincidence. I was just wondering if I'd run into Logan on campus, now that I dropped the Geology class. And lo and behold, Logan's roommate offers to turn me into a drug addict!

"Suitemate," says Mason, typing on his phone as he shakes his head. Then he looks up at me and frowns. "You know Logan?"

I blink, not sure how to answer that. But Mason doesn't wait for me to figure it out. He just winks and starts up the stairs to the side door of Main Hall. But just before he disappears, he turns his head and looks down at me with bloodshot eyes. "He'll be there for my band tonight. You should come."

5
<u>LOGAN</u>

"I shouldn't have come," I mutter as every head turns and all eyes are on me. "Looks like I'm the show here, not Mason's band."

Mason's tuning his guitar up on stage as the band gets ready. He sees me and nods, and I pump my fist and give him a thumbs up before heading for the makeshift bar at the far end of the multi-purpose room in the Student Union. I just turned twenty-one, but I've had a fake ID since I was sixteen. They serve me a cold beer, and I down half of it in one gulp. I don't drink that much—especially not when I'm training—but I'm still a bit on edge after the showdown and the ensuing publicity.

Ordinarily I wouldn't care—hell, I'm a believer in the old saying that there's no such thing as bad publicity—but this feels different from the shit I used to pull when I was a sophomore. This feels more serious, though I'm not sure why.

But then I remember what I saw in Johnson's eyes when I made that remark of how his glory days weren't that glorious, and I know I hit home with that one. It might seem dumb on the surface, but I understand how a grudge works. I understand how a man's ego drives his actions sometimes, how a man wants to strike back when he's been hit.

"Hit it!" comes Mason's voice over the speakers, and the band launches into one of their originals—which is pretty well known on campus. Mason and his band can rock the house, and I turn and lean against the bar as everyone forgets about me as they start to dance.

I'm not in the mood to show off my moves, and I hang back and tap the bar for another brew. Soon I'm three beers in, and just as I feel the creeping buzz behind my eyes, I notice that I'm not the only one who isn't dancing.

I squint at the shadowy figure of a self-conscious girl way in the back, and then I grin as my heart pounds louder than the drummer's bass. I grab two fresh beers, and then I weave my way through the crowd as my grin breaks wider, my steps get springier, my mood gets brighter.

"Didn't notice you all the way in the back. I thought you were a front-of-the-room kinda gal," I say, nudging Lara playfully as I hold out a beer.

She blinks three times, her pretty face going flush. But she isn't startled to see me. Did she come here hoping to see me? I sure as hell hope so.

"Um, I'm not twenty-one yet," she says, frowning at the beer and shaking her head.

I glance down at the beer and nod. "My bad. You're like twelve or something, right?"

Lara raises an eyebrow and stifles a smile. "That's creepy and offensive," she says.

"Lighten up," I say, putting both beers down on the window-ledge and poking her gently on the arm. "I haven't asked you out yet."

Lara can't hide the sharp intake of breath, and when I see how red she turns, I feel like a kid who just scored big-time. Suddenly all the crap with Johnson seems trivial, and all my attention is on Lara. I want her so bad it hurts, mom-jeans and all.

"Well, don't bother asking me out. The answer's no," she says after recovering her composure and folding her arms beneath her breasts. She's got a conservative blue top on, but it isn't buttoned all the way up. She left one button undone, and although it's still nun-level compared to the other girls, I'm sure she spent like an hour debating whether to do it.

"You know, playing hard-to-get only works when someone's trying to get you," I say, totally undeterred by the pre-emptive rejection.

"It's not hard-to-get, it's impossible-to-get," she shoots back, those luscious red lips curling at the corners as her brown eyes shine with play. "I don't have time in my schedule for dating if I want to graduate in two years."

"Two years? Why such a hurry? You got somewhere to go? Things to do?" I say.

She nods, losing the half-smile and narrowing her big eyes to focused slits. "Yes," she says softly. "There are things I need to do."

"Like what?" I say, clapping as the band finishes up a song. "Save the world?"

She nods again, and I cock my head and wonder if she's for real. Why the hell is an eighteen-year-old freshman so serious, so focused, so hell-bent on getting out of college?

"The world's beyond saving," she says. "But I'm going to try anyway."

I turn to her as the band starts up again. It's a wall-thumping, floor-shaking beat, and I have to lean close to Lara to make myself heard.

She starts back as I lean close, and I realize she thought I was going to kiss her or something. Immediately I back off and hold my hands up. I'm a dominant, aggressive beast in bed, but I don't come on to women who aren't interested. I sure as hell don't get a kick out of making a woman feel scared for her safety around me. Not my thing at all.

"I just want to talk," I say, smiling gently as I take a step back. "Wasn't gonna kiss you."

She nods and smiles back. Then she nods again and shakes her head. "Sorry," she says, touching her hair, which I only just notice is styled with methodical precision, like she's got a freakin' surgeon's hands. "I . . . I didn't think you were going to kiss me. I just sort of . . . I don't know. Never mind. I don't know what I'm saying. Now, what do you want to talk about?"

I hold the smile as I study her cute round face, take in the depth behind those big brown eyes. She's witty and funny, but there's also a weird sadness behind those eyes. A sadness that she's burying in this intense focus and ruthless ambition to get out there in the real world and do whatever she thinks is needed.

"Wanna get outta here?" I say, stepping close again and leaning in so I don't have to shout over the music. This time she doesn't flinch, and I shudder as I take in the clean scent of her skin.

She isn't wearing any perfume, and her body spray is delicate and subtle. No make-up other than lipgloss. Nails cut short and sensible. Slip-on canvas flats on her feet, just in case she needs to run for her life.

"Sure," she says, touching her hair and nodding hesitantly. I can see that all of this is taking some effort from Lara, that she had to fight a part of herself just to come here tonight.

I believe what she said about not having any time to date. But I also believe that she's attracted to me, that a part of her longs to break away from that ultra-focused persona and just let her hair down, let the girl in her run free, let the kid in her out to play.

"You strike me as a lot more grown-up than the other first-years," I say as we head up to the main floor of the Student Union. "Well, more grown-up than I was in my first-year, at least," I add.

We stroll past the campus store, which is about to close for the night. The grill and coffeeshop are still open, and they're packed as usual. Nobody's noticed me yet, and so I take Lara's hand and hurry her past the open entrance to the grill towards the back lawn, where there are picnic tables spread out along a bluff overlooking the river.

I frown when a couple of girls in the coffeeshop notice me with Lara. I can tell one of them just took a photo with her phone in an obviously sneaky way. I glance at Lara to see if she noticed, but she seems all up in her own head right now. It's only when I realize I'm still holding her hand that I get it.

Finally we're out behind the Student Union, and I exhale when I see that the picnic tables are mostly deserted except for a few kids vaping at one of them. I lead Lara to the edge of the grassy bluff, and we stop and look down at the dark, swiftly flowing river.

"I love how the water looks black when there's no moon," Lara says. "It's strangely comforting."

"You find black water comforting?" I say. "All right. Whatever floats your boat." She smiles and shrugs, and I turn to her and frown. "Why did you drop that class? I was counting on you to save me a seat this morning!"

Lara shrugs, and then she shakes her head and doesn't say anything.

"What?" I say, getting a sense that she wants to tell me but is second-guessing herself. "Did something happen?" I think back to that first class, when I walked out mid-lecture. "Did Professor Johnson say something to you?"

Her eyes widen for an instant, and I know I'm right.

"It was nothing," she says quickly. "He just asked that I not talk during the lecture."

"He's an asshole," I growl.

Lara laughs and shrugs. "I'm sure he means well," she says. Then she rubs her ear and looks up at me. "I saw the video," she says sheepishly. "Do you always respond to authority figures like that? Don't you play team sports, where you're supposed to get along with others?"

"Always been a loner, even when I'm part of a team," I say, narrowing my eyes when I see how quickly her mind works. "Maybe that's why I love running track more than even catching a touchdown pass. Though catching the game-winner is pretty cool too."

She nods as we stroll down the bluff towards the water's edge. "Your parents come to your games?" she asks.

My body jerks at the question, and I stare at the dark river and shake my head. "No," I say quietly. I want to say more, but it feels lame to rattle off all my family issues.

"Why not?" she says. "They must be super proud of you, right?"

"Right," I say, narrowing my eyes and staring out across the flowing waters. I turn to her and shake my head. "What about your folks? They probably tell all their friends their daughter's a genius, right?"

"They would if they were alive," Lara says after a long pause, during which I sense she was debating on whether or not to answer.

I look down at her and take a moment to read her expression. Stoic, emotionless, hard and cold even though her soft features exude an inner warmth that makes me want to hold her close. "What happened?" I whisper, touching her hand with my fingertips.

She shudders at the contact, and my body tingles with the electricity of that touch. Suddenly I yearn to know everything about her, and I reach up and delicately move a strand of hair that's fallen across her forehead.

"Tell me," I say again, stroking her cheek gently with the back of my hand. Every part of me is on fire, and I want Lara in a way that's so far beyond just sex that I can't even understand it.

She shakes her head, blinking up at me and shaking her head again. In that moment I catch a glimpse of the girl inside this strong, smart, confident young woman, and somehow I understand that she's been forced to grow up before most of us are. Hell, I still haven't grown up—and I don't know if I ever want to. But this girl . . .

"They died a year ago," she says suddenly, like she's finally decided to talk, to open up to me. "First Mom. Then a month later Dad died. They were both diagnosed with a rare genetic disease. Turned out they had the very same genetic disorder. Doctors said it was a miracle." She offers up a half-laugh and rolls her eyes. "Well, the bad kind of miracle." I see a hint of pain in those brown eyes, but one blink later it's gone. "And in case you're wondering—no, my parents weren't cousins or something gross like that. It was pure randomness. Like losing the genetic lottery or something."

"They didn't lose the genetic lottery, they won it," I whisper, my heart opening up in a way that makes me want to pull Lara close, take away all the hurt she's buried inside, make her whole again, make her mine forever. "Their genetics were perfect. After all, they made you, didn't they?"

Lara's breath catches, and she looks up at me like she isn't sure what to make of that remark. Truth is, I don't know what to make of it either. All I can think about is that Lara was made for me, and the universe has conspired to put us together.

"That's . . . that's such a nice thing to say," she stammers, curling her hair over her left ear and blushing as I caress her cheek again.

"I mean it, Lara," I whisper. "I can already tell you're special. You're special, and you're mine, Lara. You're mine."

She gasps as I run my finger down along her neck, my touch sending a line of goosebumps up her bare skin. I've said a lot of shit to girls, and by now I know exactly what to whisper to get a chick's panties off. But this doesn't feel anything like a pre-planned seduction or me aching to get my rocks off. This feels different. It feels special. It feels real.

"I . . . I don't know what that means," she mumbles as I draw close. "Oh, God, Logan. I . . ."

I place my hands on her hips and look down into her eyes. I want to kiss her but I won't. I already know that for all her confidence and poise in the classroom, she's out of her comfort zone when it comes to stuff like this. I'll bet she's still a virgin, and if so, I gotta take it slow. This shit is for real, and I can't fuck it up.

"You ever been kissed, Lara?" I whisper, smiling and holding her gaze as I keep my hands on her hips and resist the urge to run my palms farther down and cup her gorgeous bottom. I need to make sure she feels safe, that she wants this as much as I do, that she knows how serious I am.

She shakes her head and looks down, and I'm overwhelmed with a warm feeling that no girl has ever brought out in me. Is this what love feels like? If so, it means I've never been in love before, because this feels totally new. New and beautiful.

"I want to kiss you, Lara," I whisper, drawing so close I can feel her sweet warm breath on my neck. "Would you like to be kissed?"

Lara gasps again, but she doesn't pull away, and when she finally raises her head and looks up at me, I see her answer in those big brown eyes.

"OK," she says, blushing and blinking and trying to hide a self-conscious smile. "I mean yes. Sure."

I grin and shake my head at her irresistibly sweet stammers. Then I gently touch her chin, lean in close, and with all the care in the world, I kiss her, right on those tender virgin lips.

I kiss her.

By God, I kiss her.

6
LARA

My first kiss.

His lips are warm and kinda rough, but the kiss is gentle like a summer breeze. I can feel Logan's strength in his tenderness, sense that he's holding himself back in a way. Somehow I know he's doing it for me, to make me feel safe with him, to make sure I'm comfortable.

But though I've never felt safer in my life, *comfortable* isn't the right word at all. I'm so tingly my toes are curling inside my canvas slip-ons. My body's burning with a heat that's coming from inside, and I think my panties are wet just from Logan's kiss. There's a whisper of self-consciousness in my soul, perhaps even a hint of shame, maybe a touch of anxiety about what I'm doing, what he's doing, what we're going to do. But all of that evaporates like dew in the morning sun when Logan breaks from the kiss and looks at me with those green eyes that somehow back up what he said about me being his.

"That kiss confirms it," he whispers, tasting my lips once more and nodding like he's made up his mind that I taste good or something. "You *are* mine, Lara."

I feel the truth of what Logan's saying, but I resist the urge to respond. That kiss felt so good I'm still dizzy, but there's a little voice in my head whispering that I'm in deep water here and I have no experience swimming in the open ocean with the sharks. For all I know, Logan's the biggest shark on campus. And he fits the profile, doesn't he? Star athlete. Ripped like a Greek god. Can switch between arrogant prick and sweet-talking seducer without missing a beat. Ohmygod, what am I doing here?

I study his handsome face, take in those high cheekbones, that square jaw, that perfect nose. Can I believe what he says? Can I believe what I feel? Can I—

My thoughts are interrupted by the sounds of drunk students pouring out of the Student Union and descending on the picnic tables up on the bluff.

"Shit, Mason's band must be taking a break," Logan mutters. He takes me by the wrist and gestures downriver with his head. "Let's get outta here. I know a cool spot farther down the river. Come on."

He leads me along the dark riverbank, and I stumble on an exposed tree-root, crying out as I fall forward. But Logan catches me easily, steadying me and holding me against his hard body until I catch my breath. My heart's pounding as he waits a moment and then leads us farther away from the lights of the Student Union.

The laughter and chatter of the other students fades away along with the lights, and although I still feel completely safe with Logan, I've never really liked the dark and so I'm a bit on edge.

"You OK?" he says, stopping and turning to look at me. "We can go back to the Student Union if you want. Watch the band's second set. Get some coffee or something."

I rub my nose and shake my head. "I'm OK." Then I smile and nod again like I'm totally down for some adventure even though most of the time I'm totally *not* down for outdoor-type adventure. "And actually I'm curious to see this super-cool makeout spot where you bring the cheerleaders after practice."

Logan roars with laughter, sliding his arm around my waist and giving me a warm kiss on the cheek. "So I'm just a stereotype to you, huh?" he whispers. "Dumb jock who plays sports and makes out with all the cheerleaders? Thanks a lot. I feel so objectified."

I blink at the accusation—or maybe because I'm kind of guilty of the accusation. "Well, you made fun of my jeans the other day," I say.

"And yet you still wear them," he says with a wink, glancing down at my jeans and grinning like a devil. "Though I kinda like them now. They suit you."

I laugh and then widen my eyes in mock indignation. "I don't know whether that's a compliment or an insult," I mutter.

"I don't know either," he says, taking my hand as we navigate a narrow path through the bushes where the river splits off into a small stream that bubbles like a brook. "You've got me all turned around, Lara. Careful. The rocks are slippery here."

I nod and hold his arm tight as he leads me close to the stream. But then Logan abruptly stops, and I bump my nose into the hard muscle of his upper arm.

"Ow," I complain, rubbing my nose and sniffling back a sneeze. "Why did you—oh, my God! What's that?! Logan, what *is* that?! Is that a . . . a*body*?!"

"Stay back," Logan commands, gently but firmly pushing me towards safe dry ground. "Call 911, and then call campus security."

I nod and fumble for my phone. "What are you doing?"

"If he's alive maybe I can save him," Logan says, racing across the wet rocks like he's got suction cups on his swift feet. He kneels down in the shallow water and turns the body around.

It's clearly a man, and he's very big, it occurs to me as the 911 Operator comes on and I tell them we need an ambulance and probably the police. I turn away from Logan as I make the calls and then hang up. When I turn back to the scene, Logan's on his feet, staring down at the body like he's just seen a ghost.

"What is it?" I whisper. "Is he dead? Here. I know how to check for a pulse. If he's hypothermic you might not even get a pulse but he might still be alive. I know how to—"

"Stay back, Lara," Logan commands, holding his hand out and turning to me. His face is ashen, and immediately I know it's not just the sight of a dead body that's freaking Logan out. It's something else.

And when I finally get a look at the body, I understand why Logan's so scared.

Because we know the dead man.

Both of us know him.

It's Professor Johnson.

And when I look into Logan's green eyes, take in his brutally serious expression, I bite my lip and realize that my perfectly planned, meticulously organized, clean and composed life just got very complicated.

7
<u>LOGAN</u>

"It's probably not that complicated," the detective is saying to the University President as Lara and I stand near the flashing lights of the ambulance and give our contact information to a uniformed cop. "It's a nice night. He had a couple of drinks. Went out for a walk along the river. Slipped and fell. Hit his head. Boom. Done. Sad, but stuff like that happens."

The University President is always impeccably dressed and I've never seen his carefully preened feathers ruffled, but right now he looks stressed as hell. The Detective, however, is calm like a cloud. I frown as I take in the deep lines on his forehead, the savage creases around his gray eyes. I get the sense he doesn't believe what he's saying, like maybe he's playing up the accident possibility because he thinks it*wasn't* an accident and that anyone and everyone is a suspect.

Suddenly the Detective glances up from his notes and hits my gaze dead on with those cold gray eyes. I flinch and blink like a deer in headlights, and immediately I realize I just made myself look guilty. Maybe. I don't know. Fuck, does he think I had something to do with Johnson's death?

Now I'm thinking about that video from Monday where I exchanged sharp words with the Professor, and when I glance up at the Detective again, he's done with the President and is strolling over to me and Lara.

"I'm Tom," he says, not offering an official title or a last name. He does offer a quick smile, but he's cool as ice even as he pretends to be warm. He glances at his notes and looks up, first at Lara and then at me. "Logan and Lara," he says. It isn't a question.

Detective Tom asks us a few general questions about how long we were down here and if we heard anything before finding Johnson's body. Lara's still shaking, and I do all the talking even though I remember Dad once telling me that under no circumstances should I ever answer a cop's questions without having a lawyer present. A cop's job is to collect evidence *against* you. That's the job. That's how it works. It's not about who did the deed. It's about what you can argue in a court of law, Dad used to say.

But the questions keep coming, and I'm so wired with adrenaline it's almost a relief to talk up a storm. Then with a crisp, calculated suddenness the Detective stops, nods, and walks away.

"You OK?" I say to Lara, reaching for her hand and frowning when I see her tighten her fingers into a little fist and pull away. I look around, suddenly becoming conscious of how many students are standing up on the hill near the Student Union and watching the scene unfold in the distance.

Lara and I are lit up like a Christmas tree in front of the LED headlamps of the cop cars, and I glower in annoyance when I realize what this is gonna look like. Not just the whole cop scene, but also the fact that I'm standing here next to Lara, looking kinda shifty and guilty. If Detective Tom thinks I might have something to do with this, then I'll bet he thinks Lara knows something too.

"I'm fine," she says. "I've seen dead bodies before. It doesn't bother me." She offers up a faint smile, crossing her arms over her breasts. She holds the smile, but I can see her fingers still clenched into those tense fists.

The comment about dead bodies sticks with me, and I'm taken back to an old memory that's always been with me but is getting triggered by this whole scene. It's from when I was maybe ten or twelve. The cops had shown up at the door, asking for Dad. I'd been in the living room, and I remember listening from around the corner. I only picked up a few words, and it was only when the news came on the TV just then that I realized they were asking my garbageman Dad about a dead body that had been found in the city dump. They were talking to all the waste-management teams who'd done pick-ups and drop-offs that week, and I remember Dad calmly asking if the police had a warrant and if not he would like them to leave. That's when he'd made the comment about never saying a word, even if you're totally innocent. And Dad was innocent, of course. The cops never came back with a warrant, so I guess they eventually found out who did it.

I sigh and glance over at Lara again. She's shivering a little, and I want to put my arm around her and warm her up, comfort her, tell her it's gonna be OK. But I respect the fact that she's uneasy about any public display of affection in front of an audience of college officials, the cops, and yeah, most of the darned campus in the bleachers.

"I think we can go," I tell her, discreetly touching her lower back and gesturing towards the path back to the Student Union. "Come on. I think that's enough excitement for your first week of college."

She nods and we turn away from the cops, but I feel Detective Tom's attention on me, and sure enough, I barely take two steps before he calls out to me. Why did I know he was going to do that? Am I a natural born criminal?

"Yeah?" I say over my shoulder without turning my body. I make up my mind it's time to play the lawyer card, though a part of me worries that would make me look even more guilty.

I gently push on Lara's lower back and whisper, "Keep going." She nods and keeps walking, and I sigh and stop, still not turning to face Detective Tom. Now the adrenaline is leaving my system, and I'm just annoyed and want to get the fuck out of here. I can handle myself under the pressure of big lights and a big game, but this is a different kind of pressure. Winning at this game isn't as clean as winning on the track or on the field. There I'm the hero. Here I don't even know what it means to win!

"Saw you catch that winning touchdown last game of the season last year," Detective Tom drawls from behind me. "You got good hands. Great balance. Sure-footed like a mountain lion."

I nod to acknowledge the compliment, but my mind's racing as I tense up. Is he thinking about how sure-footed I was on those slippery rocks? Is he picturing my strong hands around Professor Johnson's neck, squeezing the life out of him? Or am I just freaking out? After all, it *does*look like an accident. I noticed a big bruise on the side of Johnson's head, which makes me think the guy just slipped and hit his head. Who knows why he was down here, but that's not my problem.

"Get that from your Dad?" says Detective Tom. He's a lot closer now, and I can smell clove on him. He smokes clove cigarettes? Huh. Pretty stylish for a local detective.

"Get what from my Dad?" I snap as the question only now registers as really odd. What does he know about Dad? More importantly, *why* does he know about Dad? I barely even know where the old man is these days! He left home when I was fourteen, and although he sent Mom child support and then some every month like clockwork, I'd pretty much erased the guy from my life. He did the same with us, right? Fair is fair.

"Strength. Speed. Skill," says Detective Tom.

Finally I take the bait and turn, rolling my eyes and putting my hands on my hips. "My dad was a garbage-man," I say with a snort. "Not sure if you need too many skills to pull that off."

Detective Tom shrugs, and then he flashes that tight smile again and turns away from me like that's the only reason he called me back. I'm confused, and when I turn to see how far Lara's gotten, a chill shoots up my spine when I see that a female detective is talking to her halfway up the hill to the Student Union!

"Sonafbitch," I mutter, walking as fast as I can without making it look weird. "They wanted to question us separately, see if our stories matched up. Shut the hell up, Lara. Just smile and walk away. We don't have to say a goddamn word!"

My mind churns as I wonder why President Rollins didn't step in and stop Detective Tom from questioning us without a lawyer. I thought the University President would be looking out for his students—or at least the reputation of the college. Sure, maybe Rollins believes it's just an accident and wants the whole thing to be wrapped up and closed in time for the morning news, but I'm so hopped up and wired I don't know what to think, whom to believe, whom to trust.

And then I see Lara shoot a scared glance at me, and immediately I know one thing I can trust:

I can trust what I felt before the night turned into a nightmare.

Back when the night still felt like a dream.

8

TWO WEEKS LATER
LARA

It's been a nightmare, and every day feels like I'm moving farther away from all the dreams I had when I got here. In fact I shouldn't even be here! I should already be done with college, well on my way to a PhD! I could've started college when I was fifteen, but when both Mom and Dad got sick, there was no question of leaving them to take care of themselves.

"What would you think of your genius daughter now?" I whisper to the small folding picture frame made of rough cotton that Mom had embroidered for my tenth birthday, when she could still move her fingers with precision. It's got my favorite family picture in it: Dad and Mom and me, all of us smiling in unison, somehow none of us blinking or looking away.

es us look happier than we were most of the
ut that's what pictures are for, right? So the
y is better than the reality.

ny reality right now isn't getting any better,
ough life is pretty much back to normal around
. There were whispers about Logan's publicly
asted fight with Johnson two days before the
or died, but those rumors died down simply
e they were way too far-fetched even for the
arnest gossip. Besides, although the case is
ally still open, the police haven't been around
he first few days. Even the local news pretty
lropped the story after the autopsy showed
vels of alcohol and no signs of foul play.

, that doesn't excuse the fact that I lied to the
I whisper to that happy family photo like I'm
ssion with my parents' ghosts. "Well, not real-
I told them the truth about the last time I saw
or Johnson: Up near the elevators outside the
offices. Sure, I didn't tell them about the con-
on I overheard about getting Logan suspended
ething, but that's not the same as lying, is it?"
is it?" comes my roommate Milly's voice from
ill shared space in our tiny two-person suite.

someone's at the door, and I cock my head
nder who the hell would be visiting Milly. Af-
Milly's clearly got some social anxiety issues,
barely even makes it to class at all. She's very

bright, and she gets the assignments done w
on time, so she won't flunk out. Still, if I wer
wrapped up in my own issues, I'd be concerne(
her. Though I'm no social butterfly myself, of
My phone isn't exactly ringing off the hook.

Even Logan stopped calling and texting tw
ago.

"You haven't returned *any* of my calls and
comes Logan's voice from outside my bedroo
"Hey! Lara! You in there?"

"She's in there," comes Milly's totally not
answer. I can tell Milly just wants Logan ou
presence because it makes her nervous, and s
off the bed and desperately try to decide wh
should straighten my hair or my messy bed!

I have time for neither, and when Logan bur
my tiny bedroom, I'm standing barefoot on tl
green jute carpet, my eyes wide like I just got
by lightning, my heart pounding like there's ;
party going on behind my boobs.

Logan's even taller and broader than I rem
and he's got a lot more fuzz on his face. He
shaved, it looks like, and when I see how bloods
green eyes are, I realize he hasn't slept much

Almost immediately I feel his stress like
own, and although I'd been doing my best not t
about that magical moment down by the rive
I'd just had my first kiss and the world look

and bright, seeing Logan again pulls me back to that moment so fast I get the hiccups.

I take several deep breaths and pat my upper chest to get rid of the hiccups, and thankfully it works. Logan closes the door and turns to face me, and this bedroom seems awfully small right now.

"Um, I'd offer you a seat but there's nowhere to . . . oh, sure. Go right ahead and sit on my bed in your street clothes. I have nothing better to do tonight than wash my sheets," I say, the words rattling off my tongue as I try to compose my thoughts, try to settle down my emotions.

Logan leans back against the wall and plonks one big foot—massive Converse sneaker included—right on my comforter as I try not to think about whether he stepped in something gross on the way here. I'm a cleanliness freak and a neatness nerd, and watching this unshaven man smearing his scent all over my sheets is . . . is . . .

Kinda sexy, actually.

I close my eyes so hard it hurts. Then I open them quickly because all I can think about is that kiss, that first kiss, that kiss before a dark cloud passed over our lives, casting our future in shadow.

Stop being so dramatic, I tell myself as I watch Logan fluff up my pillow and stuff it behind his back. He picks up my cat-shaped alarm clock from the window sill and turns it upside down and shakes it. Then he crosses his arms over his broad chest, huffs and puffs, and stares me down like I'm in trouble.

"What?" I say when he taps his phone pointedly and grunts up at me. "I'm sorry for ignoring your texts, OK? It's been a crazy couple of weeks, Logan! I can't get distracted from what I'm here to do! This whole thing with Professor Johnson really got to me!"

"Did the detectives talk to you again after that night?" Logan asks, losing the fake-angry expression and leaning forward like he cares about how I feel. Does he care? Do I care that he cares? Did he kill Johnson and set us up to find the body together so he'd have an alibi?

I almost choke on that last thought, and I have to turn away from Logan to hide my expression. I don't know where that thought came from, and I don't know why it's freaking me out so much. One look at Logan and I know—I just freakin' *know*—he didn't kill anyone.

And why would he, anyway?

After all, I didn't tell him about what I overheard outside Professor Johnson's office two days before he was found dead.

That sick, choking sensation comes back with a fury that makes my knees weak, and I grab the back of a wooden chair as I picture the detectives reviewing all the security camera footage from campus—inside and outside the buildings. They'd start with the day Johnson died, of course. Maybe the day before. Would they keep going, reviewing hours and hours of footage going two days back? Would they eventually find the footage of me standing outside Professor Johnson's office, clearly eavesdropping? Would they see me hurry to the elevators like a thief in the night, a killer in the dark? Or is my smarty-pants brain just going haywire with all the possibilities?

"No, no more questions after that first night," I force myself to say, turning back to Logan with a plastic smile on my face. "You?"

Logan shakes his head. "Nah. I already told them what I knew. And if they had concerns after seeing the video of me and Johnson going at it, they'd have come back for me." He shrugs and tries to act chill, but the shadows beneath his eyes tell a different story.

Only now do I remind myself that Logan's still only twenty-one. Yeah, he's a fully grown beast of a man, but he's still a kid too. We're both just kids. I may have seen both my parents waste away and die, but that doesn't mean encountering a dead body isn't still gonna be traumatic. Maybe I need to give myself a break. Maybe I need to give both of us a break.

"You been sleeping OK?" I ask, replacing that fake smile with a warm one that sparks something in Logan's tired green eyes.

He grunts like it doesn't matter, and then he stretches out his long right arm, palm upturned, fingers gently curled in a "come-here" gesture. I blink as I feel my own little spark, and as my breath catches I reach out and place my hand in his.

Slowly he draws me close to his body, and my heart's so loud I can't hear a thing. Before I know it I'm on my little single bed, leaning against Logan's hard chest, looking up into his green eyes, inhaling his musky scent.

He strokes my hair as we lie together in silence, and I'm overwhelmed by how strong my attraction is right now. I snuggle into him like a bear-cub, and he wraps those big arms around me and gently kisses my forehead.

"That night," he whispers. "I wish we could go back to that night, start over, do it again without wandering all the way to that stream. I wish you didn't have to see what you saw. You don't need to have that image burned into your brain."

"Then burn it out of my brain," I whisper up at him as I feel his hand slide down my side and rest on my hip as my butt tightens. I'm so hot for him I don't know what I'm doing, and even though I suspect that two weeks of high anxiety and continuous paranoia is contributing to this soaring need to get close to Logan, I don't care.

Logan kisses me before I can say another word, and his warm lips and hot tongue send a slash of heat right down the center of my body, perking up my nipples, tensing up my tummy, and making me so hot between my legs I want his hands in my panties.

He kisses me again, stroking my neck gently as he tastes me with his tongue. My mouth's opening and closing like a fish, and I don't know if I'm doing it right but I must be because it feels so darned good.

Slowly Logan moves his hand down my neck, teasing the swell of my bosom with his fingertip until I'm writhing like an earthworm in the sun. My nipples feel hard like little pebbles, and when Logan finally pinches my left boob, I moan out loud as the arousal shoots through me until I get wet through my panties.

"I want you so badly, Lara," he whispers as he slowly unbuttons my white blouse until it hangs open, exposing my beige bra that's less revealing than an average tank-top. "You're so damned sexy. I've been thinking about you nonstop these past few weeks. Can't eat. Can't sleep. Can't even fucking think unless it's about you. I'm obsessed, Lara. I don't know what it is about you, but all I want is to be with you right now. Nothing else matters anymore. Nothing but you."

His words melt me, and even though Logan's probably turned around by the stress of the past couple of weeks, I don't care. Spending two weeks scared to death about my little secret spying session outside

Professor Johnson's office has made me feel more alone than I thought possible—and I have *plenty* of experience feeling alone, mind you!

"The clasp is . . ." I start to say as Logan caresses my boobs through the beige satin and then run his fingers along the bra's underwire. All my bras have front-clasps, thanks to my somewhat broad back which makes getting a back-clasp fastened like playing a game of solo Twister. "Oh, you found it," I say, shivering slightly as the gentle airflow from the vents hit my bare skin. "Here, I can . . ."

"Just relax," Logan whispers, gently pulling my bra open and then groaning softly as he takes in the sight of my bare boobies, nipples pert and perky, globes heavy and ready.

I relax onto my back, and Logan kisses me between my breasts and then moves to my left nipple. He circles my hard little nipple with his tongue, and then he takes it into his mouth and sucks firmly until I arch my neck back and make a weird squeaking sound as the air escapes past my trembling lips.

Logan glances up at me, smiling with his eyes before moving to my right boob. He sucks it until my nipple is pointy like an arrowhead, and then he runs his tongue down my bare belly, lower and lower until he's kissing me just above my jeans.

He looks up at me again, and I just nod down at him. I don't know exactly what I'm saying yes to, but I know the answer is yes. That night by the river Logan said I was his, and tonight I really feel like I'm his. He's big and strong and I'm pretty sure he's done this before, but he's going so slow and gentle I've never felt safer. I wonder if Milly knows what's happening in here, but then I remember hearing the door to her bedroom close a few minutes ago, which means she's a couple of rooms away now.

Logan pops the button of my jeans, and slowly unzips me as the most dizzying heat spreads down my wet pussy. I gasp when I smell my own sex through the exposed front of my panties, and I gasp again when Logan takes a deep breath, smiles, and leans in and kisses my delicate mound through the wet cotton.

I shudder and moan, clawing at the bed as an indescribable arousal rips through me. I can feel the wetness pour from my pussy, and when Logan pulls my jeans down past my hips and off my feet, I'm so horny I'm hyperventilating.

"So gorgeous," Logan whispers, caressing my bare thighs before gently spreading my legs. He runs those long fingers along the tender insides of my thighs, going all the way up to that dark space near my crotch where that heat is driving me wild. Then he runs the back of his hand along the front of my panties, and just as my eyes roll up in my head from the rush of the contact, Logan grips the waistband of my underwear and pauses.

"This is your first time, isn't it?" he whispers up at me.

I still can't see straight, but I manage to nod.

"Do you want this?" he says, his voice peaked with arousal, tense with need. "Do you want me to be the first?"

I manage to blink myself back into focus, and when I see Logan's lean, handsome face, take in those deep green eyes that are alive in a way they weren't when he walked into this room, I know this is right.

I know I want him.

"Yes," I say, swallowing the lump in my throat when I realize what a big moment this is for me. I was forced to grow up early when my parents got sick. Now I'm growing up again, but this time no one's forcing me to do it. This time it's my choice.

Logan breaks into a broad smile that shines like the day, and I see a childlike joy in his eyes when I say yes. He smiles again and nods, and I think I see him swallow hard like this is a big moment for him too.

"Good," he says. "Because I want to be your first, Lara. Your first, and your only."

I blink three times, not sure if he's serious. He looks serious, though. He sounds serious. And this sure as hell feels serious.

But *can* it be that serious?

Can this be not just the first time . . .

. . . but also forever?

9
LOGAN

This feels like forever, I think as I look upon Lara's angelic round face, lose my vision in her innocent brown eyes, lose my mind as I inhale the sweet scent of her sex. Yeah, it feels like forever . . . and it's never felt like forever.

Never.

"I love you, Lara," I whisper as I slide my fingers under the waistband of her blue cotton panties and slowly pull them down. "I just want you to know that before we do this. This means something to me. It means . . . it means *everything* to me, Lara."

I'm saying things I've never even *thought* about with a girl, and I feel myself bonding with Lara at every level—at levels I didn't think existed! It's crazy to tell a girl you love her this quick, but it's like I've never spoken truer words in my life.

Lara mumbles something in response, but the blood is pounding so hard in my ears I can't hear a thing. Doesn't matter, though. This is about her. This is her moment. And I gotta make sure it's special . . . that it's as special as I feel inside.

Her panties go down past her hips, and I almost die at the sight of her dark triangle, her tight red slit peeking out at me through those soft feminine curls of deep brown. Her scent is clean and powerful, and I want her with a raw need that's making my body coil up like a spring, like a tiger poised in the bushes, an animal aching to be released, to do what it was born to do.

But I go slow and careful, and the act of holding myself back pulls me deeper into this surreal moment that's so all-encompassing that I'm overwhelmed with what I can only guess is love. I love her. I know it. I feel it. I see it.

I love her.

I lower my face to that space between her legs, and my lips tremble as I kiss her just above her clit. She flinches and gasps, and I kiss her there again, teasing her until her clit is stiff and Lara turns into a quivering mess. I gently hold her hips down and let her spread her legs to give me more space. Her thighs are smooth like silk, and I kiss her delicate skin and make my way back to her mound.

I'm so hard my cock is suffocating in my jeans, and I smile when I remember that I've been celibate all summer like I was keeping myself for this moment, for *her* moment. So I lower my face into her sweetness again, tasting her pussy and then driving my tongue slowly past her wet entrance until she lets out a low, whimpering moan.

Lara's so wet my chin is dripping, and I lick my lips and push my tongue into her again. I slide my hands under her smooth round ass, lifting her hips and driving into her tight pussy again. Lara groans and grabs my hair tight, pulling as I push into her again and again, curling my tongue up against the front wall of her vagina, coaxing out as much of her secret wetness as will come. I want her to be so wet that her first time is perfect, without pain, just pure magic

"Oh . . . oh, *oh*!" Lara gasps, raising her head as her eyes go wide. Then she slams her head back down on the pillow, bucks her hips up hard, and comes all over my face!

She comes so hard and suddenly I wonder if I hurt her, but when I hear her gasp and moan and buck her hips again, I know she's having an orgasm like she's never had. She's coming for me, and that means so much it's almost scary.

I lick her through her orgasm, and then I pull back and rip my shirt off. She looks up at me and gasps, and I smile down at her, caress her face, touch her lips, and then take her hands in mine.

"I want to feel those hands on me," I whisper, placing her hands on my rock-hard abs and tightening up as she runs her soft palms up along my torso. She's hesitant at first, but then I see her let go and allow herself to look at me without any self-consciousness, without any shame.

Slowly Lara brings her hands and attention down to my jeans, and with trembling fingers she touches the bulge that's all about her, all for her, just for her. I groan as even the slightest touch ripples through my cock and balls like I'm on fire, and I can't hold back anymore.

I move back and stand up in the middle of the room, unbuckling my belt, unbuttoning my jeans. My eyes never leave Lara's face, and my jeans and underwear are gone in a flash.

I want to pounce on her and make her mine with a desperation that scares me, but her sweet, innocent eyes somehow hold me in place. I stand there naked, muscled and bronzed, cock erect and hard, thicker than I ever remember it getting for any girl in my past. My balls feel full and heavy, and my pre-cum is oozing in clear beads from my cockhead.

"Logan, you're . . . that's . . . I'm so . . . I . . ." she stammers, her brown eyes fixated on my cock like she's never seen one before.

I nod and smile, reassuring her with my eyes that she doesn't need to say anything. Silently I approach the bed again, kneeling between her legs and moving closer and closer until I'm straddling her belly and she's looking up at me like she's in a trance.

Slowly I take her hand and place it on my shaft, and when her fingers curl around my cock and grip me firmly, I go dizzy from the arousal her touch brings out in me. She jerks me back and forth, hesitantly at first, glancing up at me like she's not sure if that feels good for me or not. Hopefully the way my eyes are rolling up in my head should be a clear indication that it feels really fucking good.

"That feels amazing, Lara," I mutter as she strokes me and then rubs the head of my cock with her thumb until my pre-cum drips down onto her stomach. "Oh, damn, that feels . . ."

I trail off as Lara gently cups my balls and pulls me towards her. She sits up and leans against the wall, and I straddle her and place my glistening cock between her healthy round breasts. She gasps as I move slowly between her boobs, and when I coat her nipples with my pre-cum, she grasps my shaft again and looks up at me like she's asking if she can take me into her mouth.

I grin and nod, and when she parts her lips and hesitantly takes my cockhead into her warm mouth, I almost pass out from what she's doing to my body.

She doesn't take me all the way in, and I don't push myself all the way even though I'd love that. Still, the feeling of her lips around my shaft, her tongue rolling over my cockhead, her saliva dripping down past my balls . . . it's ecstasy I've never felt in my life. I know there's no other girl who can make me feel like this, and I know that what I said two weeks ago is the truth:

She's mine.

"You're mine, Lara," I whisper down to her as I gently touch her cheek and pull out of her mouth. She looks up at me, and I smile and move back, glancing down at her soft, wet mound and looking back at her to make sure she knows what I want now, what I need now. "And I'd like to make you mine. Mine forever."

She nods as I pull her down onto the bed and line up above her, looking unblinkingly into her brown eyes as my swollen cockhead kisses her slit. She gasps as I reach between us and massage her entrance in circular motions, making sure she's wet like the rain, warm like the sun, ready like a rainbow.

Then I kiss her gently on the lips, and with a careful but firm motion, push myself into her. All the way in. All the way home. All the way to our forever.

10

LARA

I've waited for this forever, and when it comes it feels like forever. Logan enters me with a mix of gentleness and authority that makes it so clear I'm his that I can barely hold back the tears.

But the tears do indeed come when Logan kisses me again and again as he slowly and carefully pushes every inch of his thick cock into me, opening me up like a flower on the first day of spring. My mouth is hanging open as I take short, gasping breaths. I'm seeing stars and colors, hearing bells like they're in the room, smelling lavender and roses like we're in a field of flowers.

Finally Logan is all the way inside me, and he holds himself there and looks down at me, petting my hair and smiling as he flexes inside me until my pussy clenches around his thickness like it's got a dirty little mind of its own.

I smile back at him, blinking away the tears that aren't of sadness or even joy. It's just the overwhelming rush of emotion that comes from a place where emotions don't have names. It's every emotion rolled into one, kinda like the singularity of infinite density from which burst the universe after the big bang.

I almost laugh at the fact that I'm using an astrophysics metaphor to describe losing my virginity, but it feels right.

Just like this feels right.

"How does it feel?" Logan whispers.

I nod in response, my voice stolen from me, my thoughts indistinguishable from sound. I nod again, and then my eyes roll up in my head as Logan starts to move inside me.

He goes slow, pulling all the way back and then re-entering with gentle power. His cockhead drags against my inner walls in the most intimate way, and he feels so tight in me that it's like we're made for each other. Soon my hips are moving in rhythm with Logan's thrusts, like we're in a surreal dance and my body already knows the moves.

We move together like we're hand in hand in a dream-world, and waves of ecstasy roll through me every time Logan drives back in. Through my fluttering eyelids I see visions of a golden beach as the tide comes in, and I don't know if that's a metaphor or if I'm really being transported somewhere else.

It feels like day turns to night as Logan makes me his, and I get the sensation of the walls of my tiny room falling away to reveal an endless expanse of clouds. My mouth is open and I know I'm crying out as Logan fucks me, but I also feel a smile so big that my cheeks hurt.

Logan grunts as he pulls back and then drives into me again, this time a bit harder. He blinks his eyes back into focus, looking down at me like he's trying not to lose track of whether he's hurting me or not.

"You couldn't hurt me if you tried, Logan," I whisper as I raise my legs and cross them over his, just below his muscular ass. I feel my body come alive, and I know I can take anything Logan wants to give me. Anything and everything.

Logan kisses me hard on the lips, and now he goes a bit harder, building up his power until I feel his strength rip through me with each pump of his brutally strong hips. Within seconds I'm coming, my wetness squirting down past his shaft and all over the bed like I wet myself!

It feels shockingly filthy, but at the same time pure as a cloudless blue sky. Either way, I can't stop it so I just hang on for the ride as Logan fucks me through my orgasm and then finally brings himself home with a powerful last thrust that slams me into the bed and fills me so deep I dig my fingernails into his sinewy back and scream from the depths of my soul.

And then Logan comes inside me.

All the way inside.

11

<u>LOGAN</u>

I come so hard I black out, but somehow my hips keep going and when my senses return I'm still coming. I yell like a madman as my balls tighten and my cock flexes inside her as I fill Lara with my semen until she's overflowing down my shaft and past my balls.

I shout again as another blast of raw ecstasy shatters me into pieces even as the way her pussy clenches around my cock puts me back together. I'm kissing her furiously as I come, holding her as I thrust, shouting as she screams. It's so wild that I don't know if I'm ever gonna come back to reality, and when I feel my cock explode again and somehow deliver even more of my seed into her, I decide that maybe we both just died and we're gonna spend eternity in an endless orgasm.

But the best things in life do eventually end, and finally my cock is spent and my balls are empty and I collapse on top of Lara. My heart, however, is full in a way that makes it hard to speak, and I just smother my girl with my body and kiss her like I can't stop.

"Now I can die happy," I groan, hungrily tasting her lips again and then kissing her cheeks until she giggles and turns her scrunched-up face away.

"You kiss me any more and I think we'll both die of suffocation," she gasps, turning her head from side to side playfully as I try to line my lips up with hers again. Finally she stops moving and looks up at me, and I see the hints of those tears I'd noticed when I first entered her.

"Hey," I whisper, holding back from a kiss long enough for her to see what I know is written all over my smiling face. "I love you. You believe that, right?"

She blinks like a rose petal in the wind, smiles like the sun breaking through cloud, blushes like the leaves of autumn. "I . . . I . . ."

"Keep going," I whisper, grinning as I see how flustered she is from what she feels. "Almost there. Just two more words."

She laughs when she realizes I'm waiting for her to say she loves me, and it's only then that I realize Lara's turned me into a lovesick idiot without doing a damned thing! In fact she totally made me *want* to become a lovesick idiot! In a million years I wouldn't have believed that one day I'd be waiting desperately for a girl to say she loves me! In my previous life I could smell the *iloveyou* coming from a mile away, and that was usually my cue to *run* a mile away!

But now I'm *starting* a relationship with those three words?!

What the fuck just happened to me?!

And why does it feel so damned good?!

"This feels so good, Lara," I whisper. "Just lying here with you. I could stay like this forever, just holding you."

Lara sighs and snuggles deeper into my chest, and I kiss her head and enjoy the silence. I hear us breathe together. I feel our hearts beat like the same drummer is calling the rhythm.

And then I see her sneak a look at that cat-shaped clock on the window sill before groaning.

"You have class this afternoon," I grunt, sighing when I see my little genius's mind start to spin into gear. "Skip it," I whisper with a grin.

I swear I feel her body tense up like I just asked her to kill someone, and I just laugh and let her disentangle herself so she can dress. I watch her with a big grin on my face, and although she's bashful, she smiles back.

"I never thought I'd be so turned on by a girl putting *on* her clothes," I growl as my cock hardens at the fleeting sight of her butt and boobs as she pulls on a fresh set of panties and snaps on one of those super-conservative bras that somehow gets me more horny than sheer satin and black lace ever could.

Lara glances at my cock, and I see her breath catch. I want her again, but just as I slide off the bed and walk towards her, she shakes her head and puts an end to it.

"I can't miss class, Logan," she says. "Nothing's changed about what I'm here to do."

"And what exactly *is* that?" I say, frowning as I try to pull her into me and then give up when she pushes my hand away.

"Two years in college, three years in grad school, and then I join the research faculty at an Ivy League medical school," Lara says without thinking, like the plan is burned into her brain. "What are *you* here to do?"

The question hits me hard when I realize I don't have an answer. Not one that's as crisp and clean as Lara's, that's for sure. I just shrug and scratch my stubble, which is kinda itchy and uncomfortable now. "Kick ass on the field," I say.

Lara rolls her eyes, and I narrow mine.

"Can you be more specific?" she says, challenging me with those brown eyes.

I rub my stubble again, and now that I'm forced to

think about what I really want, I get that sickening feeling in the pit of my gut. "I . . . well . . . why the fuck are you asking me all these questions suddenly?"

Lara pulls on a light blue blouse and buttons her mom-jeans. "I only asked you one question," she says. "What does it mean to kick ass on the field? Which field? You play three sports, right? You want to be the best at *all* of them?"

I snort like it's a dumb question. "I *am* the best at all of them."

Lara sighs and touches the bridge of her nose again. "At Weston U, sure. No one's gonna dispute that. But you're a Junior now. Two years and you're done. What happens next? The NFL? Major League Baseball? The Olympic Track Team? What's your plan, Logan?"

My head is spinning as I listen to this freshman girl ask me questions that would make my high-school counselor proud, and I wonder what the hell I just got myself into. I'm almost pissed off about being questioned like this, but then a strange thought floats into my thick head.

This girl is special, I realize. She's got a plan for her future, and the only reason she's pushing me so hard is because I'm in that plan for her future. This is how her mind works, I tell myself. She's on a fucking mission, and if you want to ride alongside her, you better get your own damned mission straight.

So what is that mission, Logan? Football? Baseball? Track? After all, Lara's question is valid: You can't be a pro in three different sports. You're going to have to choose one, and then apply yourself with single-minded focus.

"Weston is a Division III school," I say quietly.

Lara turns to me and shrugs. "But you're a Division I talent, aren't you?"

I tighten my jaw and nod without hesitation. "Yes."

"So why didn't you get an offer from a Division I school?"

Again I'm taken aback by how this smart-ass girl is challenging me, but I rise up and respond. "Late bloomer," I say. "My dad walked out on us when I was in middle school, and I used it as an excuse to do whatever the hell I wanted—or *not* do whatever I wanted. Finally I found a release in sports, and since I was good at pretty much every sport, I played on every team." I shrug as I think back to skipping football practice because I had a baseball game, or blowing off baseball practice because I had a track meet. Not that different from now, actually. "I never focused on one sport enough to take it to the next level," I finally admit. "I always had lights-out talent. I just spread it too thin."

Lara nods, placing her hands on her hips and smiling like she's almost proud. "To be great you have to pick one thing and then put everything you have into it, Logan. I was like you in school, just in the classroom rather than on the sports field. I was good at everything from Physics to English to freakin' Art! In high school I was the best at everything, and so I decided I could do that in the real world too. But then my parents got sick, and I finished high-school at fifteen and deferred college for three years so I could take care of them. It gave me time to think, to plan, to dream of the life I wanted, the mission that called for my focused energy and attention. And when I realized that maybe the upside-down miracle of both my parents randomly getting the same genetic disorder was a clear sign that I needed to focus all my intelligence in the medical field. And so I dropped everything else and made my mind up, and I've never looked back, never second-guessed myself."

I listen dumbstruck to this eighteen-year old girl speak with the wisdom of a sage, and I can feel myself falling under her spell, falling more in love with her with every moment. It occurs to me that meeting Lara is what will take me to the next level, and when I hear her heartbreaking story about her parents and how she decided to focus on medical research to the exclusion of everything else, I try to apply her lessons to my own life.

"I always loved track," I say, furrowing my brow and rubbing my chin.

Lara shakes her head like that isn't good enough. "Doesn't matter. What are you *best* at? That's your gift to the world, Logan. I loved literature, but I was best at biochemistry and physics and genetics, and that's my mission. That's the sacrifice you have to make in order to serve the world, in order to give the best of yourself to the world. So what are you best at, Logan?"

I take a slow, trembling breath as I feel the fire burn in my belly. I know the answer. I've always known the answer. "Football," I say softly. "I've got the height, strength, and speed. And I've got the instinct to put myself where the quarterback is gonna put the ball. I make the quarterback look like a star, and that's the sign of great wide receiver."

Lara's breath catches and her face goes flush, and I grin when I see how she senses the fire burning in me. I've always had a fire, but this single conversation with Lara has focused it in a way that makes that fire feel different. That flame now feels strong enough to withstand a rainstorm. Hot enough to melt steel. Deadly enough to vaporize any obstacle.

"Then be a football player," she says. "Not a baseball player. Not a track star. Not anything else. Dedicate your life to your gift, and the universe will reward you."

I stare at her and slowly shake my head. This has been the most exhilarating hour of my entire life, and I'm blown away by the sense of purpose infused in me. I feel like my entire life is suddenly laid out in front of me:

My mission.
My career.
And my woman.

12

THREE DAYS LATER
LARA

I'm his woman, I think as we walk hand in hand through the main drag of campus. Logan's hand feels big like a bear-paw, and I can see why he's so good at catching a football.

He's also darned good at using those big paws on other, more intimate things, I remind myself just before we get stopped by a couple of Logan's buddies, one of whom I recognize as Mason, the budding rockstar.

"Yo, Logan," he says. "Heard you quit track and walked out on the baseball team. What gives?"

Logan shrugs, squeezing my hand while holding his head up, keeping his gaze steady. "Decided to focus on football. Gonna give it everything I have and see where I can take it."

"You mean the pros?" says Mason, raising an eyebrow. "NFL scouts don't come to Weston U, bro."

"They'll come for me," Logan says calmly, not a hint of bravado or arrogance in his tone. I look up at him and feel my heart glow behind my breastbone like it's being warmed by the same fire that burns in Logan. A fire that he says I helped spark.

I don't know if I can take all the credit, but clearly that conversation had an impact on Logan. Later that day he backed up his words and quit baseball and track. Then he spent the rest of the day at the football stadium, running routes all alone with just me watching from the empty stands.

Logan worked himself into a sweaty, heaving mass of rippling muscle, and there were moments he looked so magnificent down on the field that I had to re-convince myself that we were really together, that this connection that feels so deep it scares me is actually the real thing.

But now, three days later, I know it's the real thing. It's love.

"I love the confidence, bro," Mason says, fist-bumping Logan and then winking at me. "You know how to make a positive impact on a guy real quick, don't you? You got a sister I can meet?"

Logan and I both laugh, and I turn bright red as Logan kisses me shamelessly on the mouth in front of everyone. I blink away my self-consciousness and laugh again at Mason's cute comment. I shake my head and tell him I'm an only child, but then something occurs to me: Yesterday I saw my reclusive roommate Milly watching something on her laptop. When I peeked, I saw that it was a video of Mason's band, and from the look on her face, she was clearly enamored with the long-haired lead singer.

"My roommate is kinda into you," I say before gasping when I realize Milly would be mortified if she heard me set her up like that.

Mason grins and gives off a yeah-maybe-whynot shrug. "I'm doing an acoustic set in the amphitheater next Thursday. Bring her with you guys."

I nod as Mason winks at us again and then ambles his way to wherever he was going. "Where are *we* going, by the way?" I say, swinging Logan's arm back and forth playfully. "My next class is in the science building, on the far side of campus."

"I'll walk you there," Logan says.

"No, you'll be late for your class," I say firmly. "I'll see you at the Union before dinner?"

Logan grunts and smacks me on the lips, and we part ways, both of us smiling giddily. For the first time in weeks I've let myself totally relax, release the stress of the Professor Johnson incident, step away from the guilt of not telling the police that I overheard Johnson on the phone. I'm still vaguely uneasy about that, but mostly because it would look suspicious if someone saw it on camera. It wouldn't really mean much else—especially since the death looks like it was an accident. Hell, they've probably already closed the case, which is why neither Logan nor I have heard from the police about more questions.

I glance back towards Logan, and I freeze when I see that he's on the phone, his face taut as he stands still and listens like it's serious. My heart almost crawls up my throat and jumps out through my mouth as I immediately worry that everything's gonna come crashing down, that this dream will turn back into a nightmare, just like Cinderella at midnight!

Logan is waving to me, and although I see that he's calling my phone, I start to run towards him, I'm so panicked. I'm sure it's the cops calling, even though if they wanted to arrest him they wouldn't call his cell phone.

By the time I get to him Logan's running too, and when I slam into his hard body, he lifts me up and smooches me so hard I'm even more confused!

"That was the football coach," Logan says through gulps of air. "He got a call from an NFL scout out of the blue. Apparently I've been on the radar for a few teams, and when this guy saw the news that I quit all other sports to focus on football, he figured I was serious enough to warrant an in-person look! So this Saturday's game has gotta be big for me. Whatever magic tricks you pulled by coming into my life, keep 'em coming, yeah?"

I squeal as Logan whirls me around, and then I laugh when I lose a shoe in the process. We're both still giggling like schoolkids when I get my shoe back on, and it's painful to split up again for our classes.

Dinner is fun soaked in frolic, laughter and madness with his buddies, and then we spend the night in Logan's room, cuddled together after a sizzling session that makes me think I'm actually getting good at this sex thing.

Like *really* good.

Well, I think as Logan groans and collapses in a sweaty heap, panting and grinning like a dog after a run. Of course I'm good.

After all, I *am* a genius . . . ;)

13
SATURDAY BEFORE THE BIG GAME
LOGAN

"Hey, genius," I whisper, leaning over the railing and kissing my girl who's in the front row, right behind the home bench. We've got about twenty minutes before kickoff, and the team just got done with warm-ups and we're all wired and hopping about trying to stay loose. "You see the NFL scout yet?"

Lara frowns and gestures off to the left, high up in the stands. "There's an older guy in a coat, sunglasses, hat, and what I think is a fake nose sitting alone back there," she says.

I laugh at the fake nose comment, but when I see the guy she means, I shake my head. "Nah, I've seen that guy before. He comes to all the home games. Townie football fan, I think. Maybe an alum. Always in the coat and hat and glasses. Sadly I think that big nose is real, though, little Ms. Investigator. But you're right in looking for some guy in the back. The NFL Scouts like to be discreet sometimes. He's probably way out on the visitor's side or something. Anyway, I'm not worried. I just gotta do my thing and let my fate play out. And that fate stuff seems to have worked with us, right?"

"Yes," says Lara, and she looks so beautiful in the sun I almost yell out loud, I'm so fucking happy with my life. I smack her on the lips, inhaling her scent like it's a performance enhancing drug.

We kiss again, and then I let my gaze sweep over the stands, past the sea of crimson that's our school color. Then I gesture up a few rows back. "You should snag a seat a couple rows up when the game starts. You won't be able to see past the players on the bench from down here."

Lara smiles dreamily and shrugs like she doesn't care as long as she's close to me. But then Coach calls a pre-game huddle, and I kiss her again and push her towards the seat a few rows up.

I listen to the gameplan one more time, and I silently thank Coach for calling a pass-heavy game that's going to feature me. It would be a huge deal for Coach to send someone to the NFL, and I know everyone on the team has got my back. It meant something to all the players and coaches when I quit baseball and track and said I was gonna be all in on football. And it's already paying off! Just like Lara said, choose to give your gift to the world and the universe will respond!

"Where is she, anyway?" I grunt as we break from the huddle and I look for Lara in the crowd. People are squeezing in tight, and I'm worried that if Lara went to the restroom, she might not have a seat when she gets back.

I see a couple of students with painted faces, and I call out to them. "Hey, save that empty seat for my girl, will ya."

The guy blinks like he's shocked I'm even talking to him. "You mean Lara?" he says.

"Yeah," I say, smiling a little when I remember that everyone knows Lara's name on campus now. Get used to it, babe. We're gonna be front and center the rest of our lives, with both of us kicking ass and taking names. "Lara. You saw her here? Where'd she go?"

The two students look at each other and then look back at me.

"The . . . the cops took her," the guy blurts out, turning red as his girlfriend elbows him. "I mean . . . they . . . they said she needed to go to the station. She wasn't handcuffed or anything! Just some questions or something, I guess. I'm sure it's—"

He's saying something else, but I can't hear shit.

I'm already in the tunnel to the locker room, and by the time I get to the exit, I'm running full tilt.

The police precinct is downtown, not far from campus. I can get there in five minutes flat, and even though I have no idea what help I'll be, I can't not be there.

A cheer goes up through the stadium behind me, and I realize they're showing some highlights from last season—with at least a few featuring yours truly. A part of me knows this is stupid, that Lara can't possibly be in trouble. I know that she'd want me to play this game and take my shot in front of an NFL scout. Sure, the scout might come back for another game if I miss this one, but it's also possible the guy will decide I'm not serious enough to hack it in the NFL, that I have "character issues" or something—which can be a dealbreaker when it comes to the draft these days.

"Character issues," I grunt as I turn the corner and blaze past a few students on their way to the game. They yell after me, and I just wave a hand up in the air and keep going. "My character is defined by me being there for my girl. That's my fucking character, and there's sure as hell no issue with that."

14
<u>LARA</u>

Character issues, I tell myself as I fidget and stare at the empty desk in the neat office at the police precinct. They told me to wait for Detective Tom, and so I'm doing just that. It gives me some time to think about what I'm going to say.

And what I'm going to say is nothing.

Not a word.

Especially not about what I overheard Professor Johnson say over the phone: That he was looking to get Logan kicked out of school or at least suspended. If Detective Tom gets me to admit that, then given how close Logan and I are now, it might look obvious that I'd have told Logan that.

Which gives Logan a real motive.

And that gives Detective Tom enough to bring Logan in for more questioning.

Then that makes the news.

And suddenly the NFL Scouts back off, citing "character issues" with Logan being questioned about a suspicious death on campus!

No way I'm letting that happen.

I don't even care about what happens to me. I know I didn't kill Professor Johnson, and I somehow believe with childlike innocence that I can't get into trouble for something I didn't do. End of matter. My job here is to protect my man's future.

Even if I have to risk my own future to do it.

I almost smile at my own melodramatic inner monologue, but somehow it makes me feel good. It's almost like I now understand that I truly *do* love Logan. After all, I'm willing to put myself in the way of an investigation just to make sure he gets his shot at being everything he can be! That's true love, isn't it? Selfless love, not the everyday selfish kind.

"How selfish of me," comes Detective Tom's voice from behind me, and I turn quickly as fear rips me back to reality . . . a reality where I'm in a freakin' police station about to be questioned! "Can I get you something to drink?"

I shake my head, keeping my lips clamped tight. I know I should ask to have a lawyer present, but I always worry that only criminals ask for a lawyer without even being arrested. I'll stay quiet as long as I can, and if I say anything, I'll just make sure I don't actually lie.

"You aren't under arrest," Detective Tom says as he takes a seat behind his desk and focuses those cool gray eyes on me. "And I'm sorry to pull you away from the big game, but someone on my team just got through all the campus security footage from the entire week leading up to the death, and we saw something interesting." He hits a few keys on his computer and then turns the monitor toward me. "Can you explain what's happening here, Lara? It appears that you're listening at Professor Johnson's office door, doesn't it? What did you hear?"

I gulp as I see myself captured on film from above. I'm near the faculty offices, standing outside Professor Johnson's open office door, looking every bit as suspicious as I thought I would. My heart sinks, but I manage to keep my composure long enough to realize there's no sound on the video. I'm also pretty sure the faculty offices don't have cameras inside, because that would be a violation of the professors' privacy. So Detective Tom has no idea what Johnson was saying over the phone—unless he's deliberately cutting out the sound to see if I lie to him.

My head spins as I wonder what to say. I can't directly lie to the police. But I can't screw up Logan's chances at the NFL by getting him pulled back into the investigation and making it seem like he has character issues!

I suddenly feel like a scared kid again, like that fifteen-year-old genius whose big fat brain couldn't save her own parents from their fate. It feels like my world is slipping away again, like my fate is to always *lose* my fate, if that makes any sense. I'm alone again, and I just blink at Detective Tom and then slowly open my mouth to speak.

"Don't say a word!" comes Logan's breathless roar, and I leap off the chair and turn to see Logan in full football uniform, sweat streaming down his face, green eyes wide and clear, fists clenched like this is the only game he cares about winning. "They can't have anything on you because you don't fucking *know* anything!"

My heart almost rips in two, and I want to tell him that maybe I *do* know something! I know Logan couldn't and wouldn't have done it, but I'm still hiding information that could be relevant.

Now two cops run up to Logan, and he holds his hands up to make sure they know he's not a threat. Detective Tom is on his feet too, and for the first time I see the gray-eyed investigator look a bit ruffled.

"I'm fine here," I force myself to say to Logan. "You need to go play that game, Logan. Just go play the game. Please. There's nothing you can do here anyway!"

"She's right," says Detective Tom, stepping in front of me. "You're no help unless you know something we don't. Do you, Logan? Anything you want to say to me?"

I almost lose my mind at the paranoid thought that ohmygod what if Logan says "I did it" just because he thinks it might get me off the hook or something! Common sense tells me he can't do something that dumb, but the guy is all instinct and he's fired up with adrenaline and protective rage for his girl! Guys can say some pretty stupid shit with all those hormones pumping through their big muscles, and so maybe *I* should scream "I did it!" just to screw things up for the police!

Of course, that's an even dumber idea, but I feel like my intelligence is out the window. I'm all instinct now too, and in my madness I'm ready to sacrifice anything for my man—just like he's willing to do for me!

For one beautiful moment I realize that Logan's displaying the same selfless love that I just recognized in myself, and then I can't stop myself and the tears come like a freight train.

"I love you, Logan," I whisper, suddenly realizing that this is the first time I've said it to him. "I fucking love you."

My words hit him so hard he stumbles back, and then I see the love light up his green eyes. For a moment I decide it's all going to be OK, that Logan's going to kiss me, Detective Tom's going to laugh and tell us we can go, and then we'll make it back to the game before the Weston offense even takes the field!

But Detective Tom steps between us again, and that savage coldness is back in his gray eyes as he stares up at the much-taller Logan. The detective's pushing for a confession, and again I worry that maybe Logan will blurt it out just because he thinks it'll help me!

"I did it," come the words, and I recoil like I've been smacked in the face. It's only when I see Logan whip around and stare at the man in the doorway that I realize it wasn't Logan who just spoke!

"Wait, you're the guy from way back in the stands!" I blurt out, pointing at his hat and coat and glasses and big nose that looks fake.

Logan's frowning at the guy, squinting like he's trying to see the guy's face—almost like he *recognizes* the guy's face.

Finally the guy sighs, takes off his hat and glasses, and then with a sheepish grin pops out his prosthetic fake nose.

Now it's Logan's turn to recoil like he's been punched, and I gasp when I see his lips tremble and mouth the words, "Dad? Is that . . . you?"

"Yeah, kid," says the guy, clenching his jaw and shaking his head. "Look, I'll explain later. Right now I gotta talk to Detective Tom, and you two kids need to get back to the game." He glances over at the detective, who takes a slow breath, eyes us both, and then exhales and nods once.

"Go on, you two," he says softly. "We'll be in touch if there are any questions after your old man tells me what he knows."

"There won't be any questions," growls Logan's dad. He looks at his son, and I see a touching mix of pride and longing in the old man's green eyes. "But hey, just in case we don't get to talk for a while, you should know that I never missed a single game. I'm proud of you, son. Now go do what you were born to do. I got this."

15
<u>LOGAN</u>

"I got this," I growl to the Quarterback in the huddle. He's calling a play on the final drive of the game, and it's been a barn-burner if there ever was one, a total shootout that makes the wild west look like a McDonald's Playground.

We're down by four points, which means we need a touchdown to win the game. No timeouts left, which means it's all passing plays from now on—long, deep passing plays.

And that shit is my bread and butter.

I didn't think I could get my mind in the game after all the questions spinning through my brain. But Lara held my big head in her soft hands and looked me dead on like she's the power cord that charges my batteries. She told me that the great ones do what they were meant to do no matter what else is going on in their lives. They give their gift to the world even if their own world feels like chaos.

And so I stepped onto the field.

And I fucking *killed* it!

Three touchdown catches in the first half—one of which was a leaping one-handed grab that is gonna be all over ESPN even though this is Div III. Then I ran back a punt for a TD in the second half before scoring again to bring us within four, with a chance to win it at the buzzer.

Of course, the problem with kicking ass is that you get a whole lot of attention from your opponent, I think as I eye the three defenders who are lining up across from me. I'm gonna be triple-teamed on this play, and although that means some other receiver will be wide open, I know the ball's coming my way. That's how Coach plays the hot hand. When a player's in the zone, you keep feeding him the ball, no matter how many defenders are on his ass.

The play snaps and I'm gone, blazing down the sidelines like a bullet, ripping past the first defender, juking left and faking out the second defender. The third guy is still on me, though, and I'm gonna have to fight him for the ball.

The ball's already in the air, and I can sense it without even looking back. It's a high pass, so it takes some time to come down to earth. I'm one step ahead of the defender, but he's bigger and he hits hard. I'll catch the ball for sure, but holding on to it is another matter. This defender's gonna hit me like a semi-truck, hoping to knock the ball out and make it an incomplete pass or even a fumble, which would lose us the game.

But I can't think about the worst that can happen. Not now that Lara's in my life, now that she's made me believe in a future where we're both special, both gifted, both destined to bring out the best in each other.

And when I make the catch like a boss and take the hit like a soldier, I hug the ball like a baby and crash to the ground in the endzone with a goofy grin under my helmet, a steady coolness in my pounding heart, nothing but bliss on my brain.

It's just one game, but I already know it captured my fate, sealed my forever.

The best kind of fate.

And the only kind of forever.

16

THE NEXT DAY
LARA

OMG, that took *forever*!" I say when Logan finally calls after going to visit his Dad, who was just released from police custody after they verified his story. "So? Are you gonna tell me or make me wait like an asshole superstar who has no time for the little people? Not that I'm little. Quite the contrary, actually."

"Are you gonna let me talk or just keep running your mouth off like a precocious kid who's smarter than all her teachers?" comes his voice through my bedroom door, and I shriek when Logan bursts into my room, phone in hand, smile on his face.

He gives me a wet, slobbery kiss that would put a labrador to shame, and I snicker and wipe my nose as Logan flops his big body onto my tiny bed, making me bounce on the mattress.

"You would not believe what I just heard from Dad," Logan says, breathing like an excited kid. He gathers himself, takes a deep breath, and then exhales slowly like he's getting ready. "OK, I'm just gonna say it all and then I'll explain if you don't follow."

I nod and cross my legs, clapping my hands I'm so excited. I already know it's all good—obviously from Logan's expression and the fact that his Dad isn't being arrested—but also because I sense that something happened yesterday. Something that sealed our fate, cemented our togetherness, finalized our futures. It's hard to explain, but I don't need an explanation for how I feel about us and our future.

I do, however, need an explanation about Logan's dad, which is about as WTF as you can get. Yeah, he must have seen the cops come for me and then guessed where Logan was going when he ran out of the stadium. But what about the rest of it?

"First of all, Dad was exaggerating when he said he did it," Logan says. "He was there, but not really. Anyway, it was an accident. Here's what happened."

I listen like a girl-scout at the campfire as Logan tells me how his Dad saw the video of the classroom fight the first week of classes. Then a couple days later Dad ran into Professor Johnson at a local town bar with a patio overlooking the river. Dad casually asked about the video, and Johnson apparently went on a drunken rant about how Logan was done at Weston, that Logan was a dumb shit who was going to get his ass kicked out and he'd end up a loser like his garbageman dad.

"Wow," I say, biting my lip as I wonder why the cops let Logan's Dad go. "But . . . but isn't that kinda-sorta a . . . a . . . you know . . ."

"Motive?" says Logan with a head-shake and a snort. "It would have been if the whole incident hadn't been captured on the bar's CC TV." He rubs his eyes and shakes his head, smiling like he's grateful as hell. "Yeah, Dad totally got into it with Johnson. There was no sound, but they were yelling at each other on the empty patio. Then Johnson pushed Dad and swung at him. But Dad ducked and stepped back, cocking his fist but never hitting back."

"Damn," I say. "So your Dad managed to keep his cool in a fight? Pretty impressive for a garbageman."

"Wait, I'm getting to that part of the story," Logan says with a wink. "But anyway, Johnson tries to hit Dad again, and then it's like they're chasing each other across the patio! Finally Dad just dodges Johnson and runs back into the bar and gets out of the situation. End of his involvement."

"Wait, what?" I say. "So what happened to Johnson?"

"Get this," says Logan. "Johnson paces up and down the empty patio, punching the air and saying all kinds of shit which the camera doesn't pick up." Logan takes a breath and goes serious. "Then he climbs over the wooden railing onto the sloping riverbank, and you can kinda see him with his back to the camera like he's taking a piss. He finishes and zips up, but when he turns and tries to hoist himself back up onto the patio, he slips and tumbles out of view."

"Oh, no!" I say, touching my face and wincing. "He must have hit his head and fallen into the river. Gotten carried downriver and then got lodged in that stream where we found him. So it *was* an accident. Sad, but nobody's fault. Oh, Logan. That's so tragic. But also . . . I mean, it's a blessing at least that no innocent person got into trouble for an accident. Not to mention that it brought your Dad out of hiding. Why *was* he wearing a disguise, by the way?"

Logan takes a long breath, shaking his head and leaning back against the wall. He pulls his legs up, big shoes right on my comforter just like I hate.

"Garbageman," he says softly. "Also known as a cleaner."

I wait for more, but Logan stays silent. Then he sighs and narrows his eyes at me. "You know those mafia movies where the mafia runs the dock workers and the truckers and also . . . waste management?"

I frown and then my eyes go wide. "Yeah? So?"

"Waste management," Logan says. "Garbagemen."

Now I sit bolt upright and smack Logan on the chest. "Wait, your dad's in the *mafia*? Ohmygod, you said *cleaner*! Does that mean he killed people? Ohmygod, does it—"

Logan shakes his head firmly. "Not that dramatic, I'm afraid. He was one of the guys they called to clean up evidence from a job. Not like blood evidence, but paperwork and other items. Mundane shit. It wasn't that different from his regular job, he said. Mostly just taking trash bags away and making sure they were burned in the City Dump so no investigators could rummage through and find evidence. And no, he wasn't chopping up bodies or anything like that. He was small-time, but he was getting closer and closer to being pulled into serious shit, he said. The mafia handler was pressuring him, and when Dad heard one of his buddies complain about the mafia threatening his family when he refused to do something, Dad got scared out of his mind. Nobody had threatened me and Mom, but he was scared it might happen at some point down the line. He couldn't just quit being part of the mafia, and so instead he decided to just disappear. He was still small fry, didn't know enough to testify against anyone major. So the mafia would let him go without much interest, so long as he didn't pop up on the radar again." Logan shrugs. "Yeah. My dad just took off. Ran. He always sent money on time, more than the law required. But he never felt safe enough to come back to us. He was an uneducated garbageman, Lara. He thought this was the best way to keep his family safe. Just go and stay gone. It must have been as hard for him as it was for us, but I guess in a weird way he did it out of love. Selfless love that somehow hurt everyone, but was still love in a way."

I sigh as I take it all in. Then I sigh again when Logan pulls me into him and kisses me on the forehead. Love is so many different things, if you think about it.

But I don't want to think about it. Not when I can feel it. Not when it feels like this.

Yes, love might show in a lot of different ways, but this is the best kind of love, I decide when Logan leans in and kisses me tender, kisses me sweet, kisses me right.

Yup, the best kind of love.

The always kind of love.

The forever kind of love.

∞

EPILOGUE
FIVE YEARS LATER
LOGAN

"What kind is that?" Logan asks, leaning in and tasting the ice-cream sample from Lara's lips as we hover over the cool display case which is all smudgy from tiny fingerprints.

We're with our twins, Lorne and Lindsey, and we're totally holding up the line as we sample everything from blueberry to bubblegum.

Not that we need to sample anything when we could just buy the entire ice-cream parlor and use it like a dollhouse. I'm about to start my third year in the NFL, and they've already given me a long-term contract that's ten times larger than that rookie bullshit the league forces on you when you get drafted.

"Oh, wow, I can't believe it's you!" comes a voice

from farther down the line, and I sigh and prepare to sign autographs and pose for selfies even though I play for a New York team and we're in Florida. That's what you get when you end up the top Wide Receiver two years in a row. No worries. Small price to pay for the life we now have.

So I turn and flash a toothy grin as I get ready to pose, but to my astonishment the fangirls blow past me and surround my blushing wife Lara!

"Ohmygod, we *totally* geeked out on that paper you published in the Harvard Medical Review," gushes one of the girls.

"Yeah," says the second girl. "You identified the genes responsible for like three genetic disorders that scientists have been trying to cure for years!"

"And is it true you've also developed the formula for a drug that flips those genes off and effectively cures the disease without surgery or long-term care?" asks another girl.

I stare at Lara, and now I'm a little starstruck myself. I already knew what my genius wife was doing in the medical world, but I sure as hell didn't know she'd have her own groupies!

"Um, could you . . ." says one of the girls, handing me her phone to take a pic, which I do without taking it personally even though Lara's gonna hear about upstaging her superstar husband when the kids are out and the curtains are drawn and the big boys come out to play (I mean her boobs, which are milk-laden and magnificent . . . ;)).

"Mommy's a genius," I whisper to the awestruck twins, wiping blueberry and bubblegum ice-cream from their little mouths. "Let's just stay out of her way. Watch and learn, kids. Watch and learn."

And I watch as my brilliant, beautiful wife smiles for the camera and answers questions like she's the star of the show.

Which she is, of course.

And which she always was, even when we were two kids finding each other through the chaos of college.

Yup, she was always the star of my show.

The north star of my life.

The guiding light of my destiny.

The beacon that led me to forever.

∞

FROM THE AUTHOR

Sigh! Hope you liked this one!

It's always hard to see our couple leave us and drift away to their forevers, but guess what:
The CURVY IN COLLEGE SERIES is just getting started!
Milly and Mason's story is next in THE ROCKSTAR AND THE RECLUSE!
Get it now!

And in case you missed it, the DRAGON'S CURVY MATE Series awaits!

Love,
Anna.
mail@annabellewinters.com

∞

Manufactured by Amazon.ca
Bolton, ON